D0095493

Best Worst American

SS

Best Worst American

Juan Martinez

stories

Small Beer Press
Easthampton, MA

Best Worst American: Stories copyright © 2017 by Juan Martinez (fulmerford.com). All rights reserved. Page 201 is an extension of the copyright page.

Small Beer Press
150 Pleasant Street #306
Easthampton, MA 01027
smallbeerpress.com
weightlessbooks.com
info@smallbeerpress.com

Distributed to the trade by Consortium.

Library of Congress Cataloging-in-Publication Data

Names: Martinez, Juan, 1974- author.
Title: Best worst American : stories / Juan Martinez.
Description: Easthampton, MA : Small Beer Press, 2017.
Identifiers: LCCN 2016030892 (print) | LCCN 2016047377 (ebook) | ISBN 9781618731241 (paperback) | ISBN 9781618731258
Subjects: LCSH: Americans--Fiction. | National characteristics, American--Fiction. | United States--Social life and customs--20th century--Fiction. | Domestic fiction. | BISAC: FICTION / Short Stories (single author). | FICTION / Fantasy / Short Stories. | FICTION / Science Fiction / Short Stories. | FICTION / Literary.
Classification: LCC PS3613.A78645 .A6 2017 (print) | LCC PS3613.A78645 (ebook) | DDC 813/.6--dc23
LC record available at https://lccn.loc.gov/2016030892 .

The photo of Anthony Trollope in "Hobbledehoydom" on page 134 was downloaded from Wikimedia.org and was originally published in *The Writings of Anthony Trollope*, Vol. 1, published by Gebbie & Co., Philadelphia, 1900.

First edition 1 2 3 4 5 6 7 8 9

Set in Minion 12 pt.

Printed on 50# Natures Natural 30% PCR recycled paper by the Maple Press in York, PA.

For Sarah

Table of Contents

"We are all fond of the life here (except me), and there are no plans for our return."
—Charles Dickens, *Little Dorrit*

Roadblock

Lately my spinster aunt has been setting my personal posses sions on fire. I found a cup of ballpoint pens smoldering, a blob of ink and plastic by the TV. She has taken a lighter to my shelf of vintage GI Joes—their hands, feet, and arms are badly scarred. They look like casualties from an actual war. We have been living together and the strain is beginning to show.

I am thirty-five. Molly, my aunt, is fifty-three. The rest of our family died in four separate airplane accidents that took place—improbably, impossibly—within months of each other. We moved together for consolation. There were no other Macallisters left in Oviedo, Florida. We have been living together for ten years.

She hates me. She has told me so in so many words. Before the pyro bits she wrote household advice with magic markers. She wrote on the walls, by the side of whatever related to the advice. She'd write *Please clean up!!!* by the dirty plate I'd leave by the sofa. She'd write *For God's sake pick up your laundry!!!*

next to the pile of underwear in the kitchen. The messages got a little more personal after I accidentally deleted the drafts of the self-help books she was writing. She was working on two, and had most of it in hard copy, but I was downloading some songs off the computer and somehow messed it up, so that they're gone, and all she has, she claims, are the worst possible drafts. The books were called *You are Not Loathsome!* and *It's Good to be Sad and Say Nothing!*

After I deleted the files, she left a stick-figure drawing of a man with a beer belly in my bedroom. The man had a knife stuck to his head. An arrow pointed to the man, and next to the arrow she'd written *You!!!* Those messages began about six months ago. They have not stopped.

Today she drew a little comic strip on the front of the oven. A stick figure man is led to a guillotine and decapitated—the head rolls off and spurts bright Crayola blood. Next to the head she has written, *This is your head!!!* She has done a good job with the eyes (set close together), the weak hair, the double chin. I wonder if she realizes how closely she resembles the caricature. We look very much alike. We could both stand to lose a few pounds. At work, we are often mistaken for brother and sister.

We work together at a SuperTarget. We monitor inventory in a room walled with black-and-white screens. The room is the size of a closet. This continual proximity might have something to do with my aunt's feelings of anger and frustration.

The neighbors have had to call the cops only once. We keep screaming to a minimum, and for the most part try to be done with our arguments before 10 p.m.

She has covered every surface with writing. Since the markers are water-soluble, she sometimes cleans up and starts anew. Most of the new ones are either scenes of how she'd kill me (e.g., the decapitation) or, if inspiration fails, the words I hate you followed by however many exclamation marks she feels like adding.

I am not particularly fond of her right now, but I have nowhere else to go, and neither does she, and neither one can afford a place on our own, and besides we're the only family we've got so we're stuck with other. I do not wish her dead. I do wish she'd stop wishing me dead. I also wish she'd stop setting my things on fire.

The fires wouldn't worry me so much if we weren't taking care of our neighbor's kid. He looks about nine or ten, has fair brown hair and very light brown eyes, and is constantly talking, although we can't understand him. He's from Colombia. We think. The family has a map of Colombia in their living room. They moved in a week ago. No one in their household speaks English. We speak no Spanish.

We met the family as they were moving in. The kid wore a very clean but worn polo shirt and blue jeans. We saw him wear the same outfit the next day, and the day after that—Molly brought home another polo shirt that had been returned to the store and since forgotten and gave it to the father, who nodded and smiled and said something that sounded like Thank you.

Our neighborhood lies in a withered pocket of Oviedo. Barren forest to our left. Half-abandoned strip mall to our right. Boarded windows. Ghostly dogs. Every house has a dry garden with a chain-link fence. Too many people loiter on their yards drinking from oversized bottles from late in the morning to early in the afternoon. No one under seventy owns. Everyone rents.

What I'm saying is that we liked this family—young, poor, neat—though we couldn't understand a word they said to us. And they had only witnessed two outbursts, very minor altercations between my aunt and myself, so they seemed to like us too. Plus, it seemed as though they had no one else.

The father had asked me the day before. He used an awful lot of hand language, but he got his point across. He brought the kid over on Saturday. Today.

Molly soaked my razor blade in rubbing alcohol and set it on fire. (She has taken to setting things on fire that could not, I would not think, be set on fire.) The handle melted. She made sure to set the razor on a plate and to close the door behind her so the kid wouldn't accidentally burn himself.

The kid won't stop running around the living room. He won't stop smiling either. Nine or eight is a great age, the best age. He's looking at the boxes of junk sitting everywhere. Molly's crap. My crap. We're both big *Star Trek: The Next Generation* fans and have collected just about everything the Franklin Mint has put out: the Captain Picard Christmas ornament, the Borg plate, the chess set. Molly has spent quite a few of her paychecks on Thomas Kinkade prints. I've developed an affinity for Boyds Bears.

The kid loves the stuff. He picks it up. Says something in Spanish. Smiles. Runs. Picks something else up.

It is eight in the morning. We've opened all the blinds to the sun. The kid points at the drawings on the walls and smiles. He comes up to me as I'm cooking us pancakes.

He talks. Doesn't stop talking.

I have no idea what he's saying. Molly likes strawberry jam on her pancakes, I like maple syrup. I don't know what the kid will like. Has he even had pancakes before?

They keep their house very neat. Their walls are bare and clean. The four times we've stopped by we've seen the mother or the father cleaning. One or the other, while the other cooks dinner. The kid likes to color on the margins of the free weeklies his father brings from the bus stop. He pencils in happy faces and clouds and dragons by the side of ads for substance-abuse centers and sex lines. Molly gave him some magic markers. Now he colors right over the print, draws pirates over the personals.

Molly was briefly engaged six years ago. She has not been out on a date for five years. I have a hard time meeting women and tend to stutter when I do. So what I'm saying is that the odds of Molly or me ending up with a kid of our own are not good—the odds getting worse by the day. So we like this kid for a lot of reasons, not the least of which is that this is the kind we'd like for ourselves. Bright. Athletic. Beautiful.

On Saturdays I always fix pancakes for Molly and me. I usually use about half a box of the mix, but given the company I figure what the hell and empty out a whole one. The stack of pancakes is high.

We eat. I note, with some distress, that Molly has put on her control top and her black pants with the chalk marks drawn in. I go to the fridge to get the OJ and when I return my coffee is on fire. Molly is smiling. The kid looks confused but then claps his hands and laughs.

I laugh too. Molly laughs along. We haven't reached a truce, but we are in agreement as to liking the Colombian kid.

The kid keeps talking.

Molly nods and smiles, pretends to agree, to understand what he's saying, then says that we should get going. That I should hurry the hell up and dress and get ready. I thought she'd want to skip it this Saturday. I ask her about the kid and she says we'll take him along, then lights my spoon on fire.

On Saturdays Molly likes to drive to the Orlando airport to distribute her literature. She makes the pamphlets herself. She has a very creative side, which she has combined with unfortunate results with her religious side. It all began to get messed up shortly after the violent and unlikely destruction of our entire family.

She believes that you have to accept Jesus as your lord and savior. She also believes that Jesus has set up a committee to run things on earth, which is kind of like the Illuminati or the Masons—she says that the committee is called Pragma (short for Pragmatists). It is made up of very old men who wear pinstripe suits. They are capable of magic, know incantations, can make household pets speak for days or weeks at a time, and are all chaste. No Viagra for them. They are old and pure and the problem is that some of them are senile. They've been living for centuries. They used to keep things running smoothly but are having a harder time of it now. Hence why the world is in the state that it's in, and why all these people are running around behaving like they do, why countries are at war, why the past is in all regards preferable to the present, and it also explains how thirty-four Macallisters died in four months, thirty-three aboard planes, one in the airport parking lot. In her pamphlets she goes into the workings of Pragma at more length. She also asks for contributions and suggests that while we really should not question God's design, we should see about replacing some of the more senile members of the committee, so that maybe the world will right itself.

She cannot afford a pinstripe suit but has fashioned a caricature of one with black clothes and paint she picked up at an arts and crafts store. She has made one for me, too, and I have to wear it and distribute the literature and talk to any potential convertees. I have to do it else I don't get any driving privileges. She sometimes lets me drive her '85 Corolla, but only during the weeks I've agreed to go with her to the airport.

So we drive, Molly at the wheel, the kid in the back, me riding shotgun. The kid keeps talking. I can't understand a word he's saying but don't care. It's like listening to sunshine.

★ ★ ★

We pass the security roadblock, show our permit, the kid smiling and looking like waiting in parking lots was the most exciting thing in the world. Everything's new for him. This whole town strikes him as a miracle. I caught him staring very intently at the bright green of the highway signs as we drove in, the billboards, the fast-food signs on their impossibly high stilts. I'm trying to remember if I ever felt that way. As if everything was new.

Of course I did. I must have. Didn't everyone? I didn't, or don't remember.

But as we're driving into the airport I'm thinking that this is how everyone should deal with everything, every day. I'm filled with a hazy sense of peace, joy, tranquility. The light in the parking lot is dark and gray and cool. The feeling fades as I put on my jacket with lines drawn in crude and shaky. Molly hands me my stack of pamphlets. We will be here for about five hours.

We lose the kid after the first. He had been running in circles for half an hour before getting tired. We thought he was still sitting by our side when we found that he was missing. Gone without a trace.

We run up and down the terminals. We start at Virgin and work our way up. We look for hours, Molly in tears, her pamphlets scattered on the floor somewhere around British Airways. We run up and down the airport. I suggest that we talk to someone, run a message over the intercom, but Molly will not allow it. She believes airport officials are in league with the old men in the pinstripe suits. I'm trying to think of what to tell the father, that we lost his incredible child, and I dread the conversation mostly because I'd have to bring in someone to translate, someone from work, anyone, and I cannot imagine the grief or the pain—cannot imagine the feelings themselves, but what I really do not want to, cannot really conceive is how you'd translate grief, or pain, how the words would hop. Of course we'll have talked to the police first. And Molly or not we have to talk to someone at the airport. Soon. I have been running with my hands on both sides of my face. I have been pulling at my ears. I just realized this. I put my hands down. I keep running. I run and run and look for the kid and notice that I'm rubbing my hands together and crying. Molly's by my side. I put my hands down. We're holding hands. We stop. We hug. I tell her that it'll be OK, that we'll find the kid, that he couldn't have wandered off all that far. I pat her back.

Molly has set my jacket on fire. I let out a very high squeal, push her out of the way and take off the jacket. Stamp it out on the rug. Keep running. Molly seems to have twisted her ankle. She has not gotten up and is pounding at the rug and screaming my name.

They'll find pieces of him. Arms. One leg. One foot in one sock in one foot, neatly severed. Or whole but dead, a few drops of blood dotting one nostril. Or alive but horribly violated. Or not horribly violated but burned, hurt, scraped, bleeding, broken. Apparently my hands have made their way back to my ears. I pull them, thinking, Stop, you'll tear them off. Or they won't find him. They won't find anything. Or they'll find the polo shirt. Or nothing. Nothing. And me and Molly'll go to jail. We'll be the prime suspects. We'll deserve whatever they give us. We lost him. We're as bad as whoever finds him and does terrible, terrible things to this incredible kid. We'll find him. We won't. I keep running. My hands have apparently decided to cover my mouth. My mouth was making a kind of keening sound. I'm sorry. I'm sorry. We'll find his torso and nothing else. He's lost. Gone. Dead. Because that's what happens when you're small and lost and you've got the wrong people taking care of you. We're wrong. We're so wrong in so many ways and now he's dead.

Roadblock ★

I had not believed myself when I told her that he couldn't
have wandered off too far but it was, after all, true—there
weren't many places he could have gone to. I find him in the
As. The Avianca terminal.

He's talking to a very young woman with skin the color
of teak, eyes gray and somehow metallic. Around the two
there are others like them, old and young, carrying nothing
or oversized cardboard boxes sealed with duct tape or back-
packs. They hug. They stand in circles. They talk on cell-
phones. They talk to each other in the same bright musical
inscrutable tongue of the kid. He points to me. I wave and
walk closer.

"So you're the babysitter," she says.

I nod. I try to talk but stutter.

"He was asking me how to buy a ticket back," she says.
"Says he likes it here but felt like going back for the weekend.
Bright kid. He was telling me about the roadblock."

"I know. It was pretty fast this time. Guess they're relaxing
it a little bit." I get it all out really quickly and don't stutter too
much.

She looks at me for a long time.

"I mean, they looked at the trunk and asked for IDs but
that was it," I say.

"No. The one in Colombia? The retén?"

"I don't speak Spanish," I say.

"His whole family got killed. All his cousins, his uncles. At
a roadblock. They were on their way to a picnic. The guerillas
stopped them along with about a hundred other cars. They
stood by the side of the road. Stood for hours. You didn't know
this?"

I shake my head. She continues.

"He says it would have been all right if the military had not
intervened. There was gunfire. Most of the people by the side
of road got mowed down."

9

The kid holds the woman's hand. He hasn't stopped smiling. "That's why they moved?" I say.

She turned to the kid and asks. The kid answers.

"No. That's another story."

"So how come he didn't. You know. How." I'm having a hard time of it. "Why is he still alive? How did he make it out of the roadblock?"

She turns again and asks.

"He was short," she says, "and lucky."

The kid lets go of the woman and takes my hand. We shake. The last time I shook a woman's hand was—I can't remember. I can't remember the last time I was this close to anyone that pretty. I let go because you cannot keep shaking a stranger's hand no matter how much you want to.

We wave good-bye and find Molly, still on the floor, right by the embers of the jacket. I pull her up. She cheers up when she sees the kid. I want to tell her about the conversation I'd just had—about what the kid had gone through. But what could it add? What could it do for Molly? What would it tell her that she didn't already know? It'd just confirm her insanity. The old men in charge had messed up not just here but in South America. Of course. Didn't I know, from reading the literature, that it was worldwide, this conspiracy? And besides, it didn't matter, this information, not with the kid by our side—something horrible could have happened, and it didn't. He had been missing and now he was not, and Molly and I are for the moment not acting terrible to each other. She's happy. So am I. So is the kid.

We make our way out of the airport and into the light of the outside world, into the fortress of the parking lot, the three of us walking very close together. We hobble to the car and drive home.

Strangers on Vacation: Snapshots

They stand three and a half blocks from the Eiffel Tower and look as though they hold the monument in their hands.

They are at the beach, holding hands.

They are at the beach, not holding hands.

They are at the beach, and one is missing.

They are at the beach, their backs to us. They are staring at the sea. The missing one has returned with a boogie board.

They are at Disney World. A man or woman in costume is with them. The costume is not immediately recognizable as belonging to the pantheon of Disney characters. It is a weevil.

They are at Six Flags. The same man or woman in the weevil costume is with them.

They are at the beach, buried to their necks in sand.

They are at the beach, a treasure chest in front of them. The weevil holds a metal detector, the others shovels.

They are at Disney World, wearing Mickey or Minnie Mouse hats according to their gender.

They are at the beach, wearing the same Mickey/Minnie hats.

They are at the Hard Rock Cafe, rocking hard.

They are at Planet Hollywood. The weevil is with them.

They are at Coney Island, riding a roller coaster, eating hot dogs, winning prizes, getting tattoos.

They are at Mount Rushmore—out of focus, but behind them, atop the head of Washington, one can see a gripping struggle: A man wearing tails, a monocle, and a cape is pushing down a man in a gray suit. They are fighting to the death! The man in the gray suit hangs by the nose. Is all hope lost? Clearly not—that man in the gray suit has steely determination. He will prevail. Atop Roosevelt: the man in the weevil costume.

They are at the beach again, badly sunburned.

They are in a living room. Is it their living room? It must be. They're home. The man or woman in the weevil outfit is in the kitchen, fixing the family pancakes.

Machulín in L.A.

I'm not married. I've attended thirty-seven weddings this year. I'm on my way to the thirty-eighth, with the bride in tow. Mirabela, the bride, will be marrying my cousin Chapulín. I'm going with her to Los Angeles. We sit in an airport bar, in Orlando, waiting for our flight. Mirabela is twenty-five and an intern like my cousin. They met at UCLA, and in their white coats they palpated the brains of small mammals. From what my cousin has e-mailed I know that they are both considering the field of neurosurgery. Her hair is short, bright-red, and intense. Her eyes are pale blue. Her skin glows against her neon blue top and dark jeans. She's Argentinean but has lived in Los Angeles most of her life.

Mirabela has drunk four Long Island Iced Teas. She orders her fifth drink. She has raised her bright shining arm and ordered another. I have not had a drink in a year and a half, since the summer of 1998.

I have no desire to attend this wedding. After the thirty-seventh I swore off weddings—the brides, the toasts, and the nuptials all offering further confirmation of my failure—but Mirabela happened to have a conference in Orlando a few days before hers. My cousin asked if I could accompany her— if I would attend the wedding—since relatively few from our side of the family would be able to make it. I said that I did not mind, though of course I did. He offered to front me the plane money. When I said that No, I couldn't take it but would of course not mind helping out, he did not insist. He should have insisted. I would have taken the money. I work at a goddamn Blockbuster. I hate flying. I hate leaving. Our flight leaves in twenty minutes. Mirabela, the bride, is a graceful drunk.

We have not said much to each other. We have very little to say.

"Chapulín tells me you made a movie," Mirabela said half an hour ago.

I grunted. I have very little to say about the movie.

The pudgy waitress, in the black shirt with the flower print, exchanges Mirabela's empty glass for a full one. Behind the waitress two men argue over the remote. The winner has switched to the Sci-Fi channel. The back of his shirt reads, *Be Seeing You.* I recognize kin. I don't have to look at the front of the shirt to know that it will show the outline of a penny-farthing bicycle. I scratch my beard—I'm five foot four: like all short men I have grown a beard. I weigh two hundred and fifty pounds. Like all fat men I wear a cape. Like all fat men who have failed I wear a cape or a cloak.

She has ten minutes to finish her drink.

She's half done. She should look debauched or seedy in her drunken state but does not. She looks radiant. Her skin shares the same coppery intensity of her hair and her neon blue top. She's all about that neon.

"This movie you made," she says, "you must like movies a lot."

I have never been to L.A.

I grunt. I'm halfway through thirty hot wings.

I grunt and nod. In ten minutes I'll be flying to L.A. with a neon angel.

"I've been to thirty-seven weddings this year," I say. "I have this notebook with all the photographs."

I pull out the Mead book from my Jansport bag. She flips the pages with a deliberate delicacy. She's overcompensating for her drunkenness.

Mirabela of the bright and impossible skin gulps down the rest of her alcohol. She flips to the end pages of the composition book, where I have pasted photographs of telephone wires and blue skies.

"These are really pretty," she says, placing her neon hand on my thigh.

She's drunk. She's leaning. She could fall.

"I took those," I say. "We should go."

Her hand rests on my thigh. She could be Jean Seberg, she's so pretty.

I always wanted to direct. I majored in film. In the gray bubble of my failure, I see that what I loved most was imagining how certain key parts of my life would look like when captured in film.

Mirabela leaning on my thigh—that moment belongs on film.

I lived in Bogotá for four years before returning to Orlando to finish my degree. I mention it only because it was there that I was hit by another moment that belonged on film.

I wore Wayfarers and was about to walk past the cathedral by the Centro Granahorrar. The sun was about to set. The light had turned thick and golden. I took off my sunglasses and turned my head to the doors of the cathedral, which opened as I passed. Pallbearers walked out with a coffin. It could have happened in slow motion. It could have happened in a Hong Kong film.

I tried to replicate the moment in our movie. We shot it in slow motion. I told the actor where to look, how to look. It came out wrong. In the movie it looks gimcrack and clumsy. In life it had been smooth, glorious, and filmic.

What was supposed to be funny wasn't. What was supposed to be sad wasn't. We had poured a year of effort into it. We had run up credit cards. The movie had been swallowed whole. I want nothing to do with my bastard child.

"We should go," I say again. "We'll be late."

I hate flying. I hate being late. I hate my cousin for marrying the lovely woman leaning on my thigh. She stumbles to her feet from the stool and leans in close. The men by the TV watch *Mystery Science Theater 3000*.

"Wait," she says. "Before I forget. Let's meet at seven. We have to meet at seven. Is there anywhere you're going? Any sights?"

My movie.

"The Museum of Jurassic Technology," I say. "I want to visit the Museum."

"Let's meet at seven over there. I like your cape."

I shake my head. She has pulled the edge of my cape to her nose.

Mystery Science Theater 3000 is showing my movie. The silhouettes running along the bottom edge of the TV screen are making fun of my movie. I can't blame them. We tried. We tried to make it good and could not. We were not good enough to make it good.

The man in the *Be Seeing You* shirt laughs. The man he scuffled with also laughs.

We're late. Our flight is leaving. I'm a failure.

"Don't tell Chapulín we're meeting," she says. "He can't know we're meeting. So don't tell him. I hate flying. I need another one of these."

I'm Hank Quinlan running down the bottom of the bridge in *Touch of Evil.* Marlene Dietrich asks the camera if it matters what you say about people. The man in question is dead and floating.

I'm sinking. We're flying.

She grabs my hand every time we hit turbulence. I hate flying. I hate turbulence, but I don't hate it so much on this trip.

If the plane shatters and we're spilled into nothing and die, it seems not so bad with her in tow. Her beauty muffles the terror.

She dings the stewardess for a beer. She pulls a pill from a murky orange case and downs it with the beer. She reaches for my hand and sometimes misses and hits my thigh. Then she falls asleep on my shoulder. Mirabela is not nearly half so graceful in her sleep and leaves a discreet spot of drool on the cape. I fall asleep as well. I wake up from a dream where I am covered in fine pale dirt. I brush it off when I wake.

We're landing.

Chapulín waits for us. He waves—a tall muscled bastard. He hugs and kisses his bride-to-be. He hugs me.

I'm happy to see him. I stayed in his apartment and mooched off his family when I lived in Bogotá. He had been doing his pre-med. He smoked then. We drank. We drank like there was no tomorrow. He buried himself in his studies. I slacked off.

He still drinks. At least I've stopped drinking. At least I've stopped smoking.

He drives me in his SUV and drops me off at his sister's. Chapulín's sister hugs me. Other cousins hug me. Chapulín's sister's illegitimate child hugs me. I'm thinking of how I'll be meeting the bride at seven.

Light falls thick on the city. You walk through it like you'd walk through water. You'd think the light would wash away the grit on the signs, the low cloud of fumes. It doesn't. I stumble into Culver City. Behind me the family waves. I say that I am off to see the sights. I could take a nap. I pass by a shirtless black man and his pit bull. The pit bull lets me pet him. The man welcomes me to L.A. I'm expecting anger and beautiful women. I'm expecting gangs. Instead the man tells me what bus to take to get to the Museum. He compliments my cape. I walk away, sweating.

I pass by three Indian restaurants and stop at the fourth. I spoon mint chutney from a jar on the table, chomp on the orange skin of a tandori chicken, and realize that I'm jetlagged. I step into the aggressively ethnic streets of Culver City—Mexican locksmith stores, Colombian and Guatemalan calling-card stores, more Indian restaurants.

When I find the bus stop, I photograph the wires overhead. The camera clicks and I hear a faint delayed echo behind me, and assign the sound to another camera. I turn around: no one's there.

My watch says it's five in the afternoon. I can't remember if I adjusted the time. The Museum of Jurassic Technology is smaller than I expected. A pale blue flag hangs over its door. A small metal lip curls over an empty fountain. I knock on the metal door. I'm let in. I see no one.

Tomorrow I'll miss a bus and strand myself for an hour on Sunset. I'll be wearing my Jurassic Technology T-shirt. I'll walk by Mann's Chinese Theatre. I'll turn to find the Max Factor building, boarded and abandoned, then a Freemason temple, also boarded, crumbling, and abandoned. I'll wander into a Jaguar dealership. Three improbably good-looking men in make-up and headsets will be improbably nice to me. They'll offer me coffee and give me directions. I'll spend the afternoon at the Getty center.

L.A. should be seedy, unfriendly, and full of broken dreams. I'm a failure looking for failures. I fail in finding them. I have dived into the city and am looking for William Holden floating above me.

Instead, impossible light, improbable smiles. From the Getty center you can hardly make out the city in the smog. Pollution makes it a paradise about to vanish. It shouldn't be pretty but it is.

My expectations. My head. The knot of desire in my guts. The ghost of the kiss at the Museum.

She's waiting for me in the Museum of Jurassic Technology, at the Sonnabend exhibit, in a blouse tinged with the powdery blue of the L.A. sky. The darkened room holds dusty letters, faded photographs, a wedding dress from another time. Between us sits a record player encased in a glass shelf. The room holds the earthly possessions of an Argentinean opera singer.

"You're early," she says.

"You too," I say. Behind her the photograph of Madelena Delani glows faintly. I can spy Madelena's face in the dark of the room. Mirabela's face glows with the same unsettling intensity I spied in the airport. Madelena has tucked her hair into a bonnet for the photograph. They could have been twins.

I remember *Vertigo:* Jim Stewart looking at Kim Novak looking a painting of herself. The jet lag will not go away. I could be falling.

"They say we had an opera singer in our family," she says. "It could have been her. I've lived here most my life and I've never been here. I'm glad we settled on this place."

My throat has turned to dust. I can neither articulate nor grunt my agreement.

"She could be my great-grandmother," she says, looking at the photograph. "I've lived here most my life. I haven't visited Argentina in forever."

"You look very much alike," I say. "She's very beautiful."

"You were very sweet to have said yes. You could have said no. Chapulín is lucky to have a cousin like you," she says, and presses a red button by the faded wedding dress and the photograph.

The room grows darker. Light blooms from the glass shelf that separates us. An aria descends from concealed speakers. Madelena Delani sings through the static of time. She would have sung the same song deep in the Amazon in a floating barge out of Herzog's *Fitzcarraldo*. She would have sung the same song to sailors and businessmen who were dark and short and lonely and overweight. We would have sat and stared at her across the chasm of the orchestra pit. We would have listened.

I walk in the darkness to where Mirabela now stands next to a faded dress. My head brushes hers. She turns. The song stops. I kiss her. She slaps me. The lights in the room flicker, struggle, fade again, return. Mirabela's face no longer resembles Madelena's. Mirabela is seriously pissed off.

"Asshole," she says. "You fat asshole. Cabrón."

"You said that you wanted to," I say. "You said you wanted to meet me here."

She slaps me again. The room freezes into cold segments of strobe light. We turn from the ignominy of my misunderstanding to find the man from the airport bar, still wearing his *Prisoner* shirt. His camera clicks and whirrs—he's out of film.

I stumble toward him. In the small dark chamber the silk-screened print of the bicycle glows blackly against the neutral field of his shirt and the dark of the exhibit. I fall and hit my head against the sharp edge of a diorama. I've fallen face first and have dislodged a sign. *Obliescence: Theories of Forgetting and the Problem of Matter.*

Mirabela hustles me back to consciousness with worried little slaps. Her blue eyes shine in the unnaturally bright confines of the room. They've turned on the lights. The mystery man has vanished.

"I tore down a sign," I say. "I'm sorry."

"You shit," Mirabela says.

"I'm sorry," I say.

"Cabrón," Mirabela says again. Her eyes will not stop shining. They are unnaturally pure, bright, and blue. "You shit." Her eyes will not stop shining. "Chapulín doesn't have any friends here. I was going to ask you to do a little bachelor thing for him. Take him to a strip club. Asshole."

"I'm sorry," I say. "I didn't know. I'm sorry."

Those eyes.

Mirabela leans in. She tries to pull my fat body upright. She can't. Her eyes—she leans close to me. Her eyes look down from a place of infinite beauty. She has never been so close to this slumped and heavy-breathing incarnation of failure. Her eyes look down from a place of infinite coldness and purity. She tips my chin with her neon hand. Her face leans closer.

We kiss.

My Seberg. My Jeanne Moreau.

We kiss. She kisses me. I kiss her back. We kiss.

I stand up. She brushes a tear from her face. She smiles and hands me a hundred-dollar bill. "Somewhere fancy," she says.

"Nothing too seedy. My brother will go with you. He'll drive you guys. He'll know where."

"Okay," I say. "I'm sorry."

I take a nap. I dream again that I'm covered in fine white ash.

Ricardo, Mirabela's brother, awakes me. He is tall, lean, and fit, and long-limbed like his sister. He looks like his sister. We pick up Chapulín and take him to a strip club, where girls in their unearthly twenties move with no affect, their smiles frozen, their breasts for the most part unenhanced. The hard-on is real but the experience itself is not.

I drink poorly-brewed coffee. They drink beer. The girls gyrate. We leave with our hard-ons and with none of the money that Mirabela gave me.

We drop Chapulín off. Ricardo drops me off. Ricardo should not have been driving, but I don't drive.

"Nice to meet you," he says.

"Nice to meet you," I say. "It was fun." It wasn't. It was. It didn't feel real.

"It's funny, your name, Machulín. You're Machulín and he's Chapulín."

"Nicknames," I say. "My name's actually Josué. His is Jorge."

"I knew that," he says. "I knew his. Jorge."

"A lot of jays in our family. Tons of us birds. There's five Juans and one Joan and a couple of Josés and some Jorges."

"Damn."

I shrug. All Colombians shrug the same way: when we shrug we're asking, What can you do?

We're inside a mission-style chapel. Mirabela looks lovely. Chapulín looks happy. He should have crumbled into a pile of pale ash, and that pile should have been scattered by the wind.

I would have taken his place. Two priests run through the ceremony. They switch off tag-team style. One speaks in English.
The other one also speaks in English but switches to Spanish at different parts of the homily. The one that speaks only
in English looks Latin. The one that speaks in perfect English
and in perfect Spanish looks like he's Irish-American.

I'm touched by the easy and graceful bilingualism of the
ceremony. This chapel strikes another *Vertigo* chord. It too
adjoins a cemetery. Could they have filmed it here?

No. They set the movie in San Francisco. So no, maybe
a set in Culver City or on location, the actual city, but they
would not have used an L.A. chapel. We pass a statue of a man
named Sepulveda. We pass children wearing paper skulls on
their way to the cemetery.

That's it. They're married. Bastards.

We're shuttled to the reception. I'm seated next to a very old
man whose blazer pocket bristles with ballpoint pens. The
other jays flock the table—the Juans, the Josés, the Josúes.
Most I know or knew before. I'm glad to see them. I'm introduced to another Colombian living in Orlando, a distant rela-
tive who shuffles and coughs and doesn't look at me in the eye:
I dislike him immediately. Another jay.

Mirabela and Chapulín step to the center of the hall. The
bride waltzes with her father. We're asked to form a line to
dance with the bride. I do not join the line. They waltz. The
men dance with Mirabela, the women with Chapulín. Each
is given a safety pin. They pull bills from their wallets. Before
they dance they pin a bill to Mirabela's wedding dress. I think
of Madelena Delani singing to no one deep in the Amazon.
Herzog sang to no one, too, as did Welles. No one expected
much from *Touch of Evil*. *Fitzcarraldo* cost more than it
was worth. Herzog turned to documentaries for German

television. Welles voiced-over a massive planet in *Transformers: The Movie*. We know we've failed when we have no money. But Herzog's movie was passable, and Welles' brilliant, and mine was neither; mine failed, and the only money that trickles in comes from *Mystery Science Theatre 3000*'s residuals. My aunts pin bills to Chapulín's tuxedo. I'm happy for them. I'm happy for all of us. The old man sits with me at the empty table. He introduces himself. I forget his name immediately.

"I'm a Mason," the old man says. "Your cousin's a member. I'm representing the organization."

The old man had nothing better to do. He must wander from one wedding to another.

"I didn't know that," I say. "I didn't know Masons had representatives at weddings."

The old man nods.

"I didn't know my cousin was a Mason."

The old man looks away. How many weddings has he attended? Isn't it a secret? You're not supposed to tell people you're a Mason.

The man in the *Be Seeing You* shirt stands at the other end of the hall. I walk toward him. I stumble onto the waltz line and dance with the bride. Mirabela smiles. She's so happy. She's so fucking happy. I smile. I can't help it.

Someone photographs us. The room buzzes with flash strobes, and with the clicks and whirrs of cameras—they're documenting everything. I step off. Someone else dances with the bride. At my table the old man sits alone. The man from the museum reaches for my hand. I shake it. I want to punch him. He offers me a beer. I tell him I don't drink. He finds me a Coke.

"This one's the last," he says. "The thirty-eighth. The thirty-eighth's the last. We're done. It's a wrap."

"Why have you been following me?" I say. "Why have you been following me to weddings?"

"I'm a fan," he says. "I liked your movie. I'm in film school? I thought you had some nice moments in there. Some pretty cool things in the movie. I mean, it's rough? But still." He's younger than me. Thin, but growing heavy. "Anyway," he says. "I'm sorry. It's a project. Like a documentary?"

"All stills?"

"Yeah, but we string it along, you know. Dissolve dissolve dissolve. Do a *Jetté* thing on it. It's all sort of Luc-Godardian. Film on filmmakers. Or film on people who love films. Look." He pulls out a sheaf of photographs. They're me. I'm looking at a fat man wearing a cape. I recognize the backdrops. The man wearing the cape is a mystery. He's a failure. I don't know him. He's not me. He is. I do know him. He photographs wires, leans into the sky for a better angle, grows old while making a record, something that stays put, something that moves, singing to no one, singing alone, singing to one film student.

I return the photographs and walk away, fly home, the edge of my cape pinned to the hills of L.A. and unfurling from one edge of the continent to the other, a thin black ribbon drifting to earth and settling soundlessly over Orlando.

Would the film student document it? Would he shoot the thin line bisecting the country? His project is done. We're done. I land to find a child no fatter than my thigh clicking away with a Barbie digital camera. She's documenting the gift shop, its magazines, T-shirts, and paperbacks. She's documenting the Disney store, the Warner Bros. store, the terminals, the empty bar with its stools upturned and resting on top of the tables, the bags, the people leaving and those returning. She zooms in on the fat man and clicks away at his bags, his shuffle, his heavy return. The fat man in his cape. I smile at the little girl with the camera. We say we are doing this for no one, that we're doing it for our own sake, but that's not quite true.

She keeps clicking as the fat man floats through the airport window. Departure dissolves into arrival. I think we should dolly far from here, or cut or fade out, or wait for the next scene.

On Paradise

You don't have to write back if you don't want, either one—if you don't that's fine, that's OK—but if you do want or even if you don't and you got this and it's the right address then please *please* just let me know. Like maybe through a friend? Or through Uncle Carolina, though he says you haven't been in touch for years?

Or Craigslist?

Or you could leave a feather, a headdress, a rhinestone—anything, some sign you are who I hope you are—up at Jim the manager's office, at the place I'm staying, which from the looks of it you'd think would be scary, on Twain and Paradise, but even though the room smells like cigarettes and the courtyard's full of these ladies who are all skin and bones and who have some very clear chemical dependency issues, and even though you hear sirens all the time, and even though it's like *Cops*, the show, mostly because it is *Cops* (the video crew comes around with the police: bright lights, video cameras, the ladies and the cops bantering, everyone weirdly pleasant to each other), and even though I have been offered drugs six times, this place is actually not as bad as you would think, and Jim is actually a nice guy, and I'm running out of time. They need me back in Orlando at the pet store. Everyone is wigging out over cricket portions.

I am at a Budget Suites of America that lost its franchise rights, so it is just Suites of America if the plastic sheeting over Budget hasn't fallen off—but I think if you write to either name it should still get here. It is the address I wrote down for you. Mail gets delivered now. Jim is new. He is turning things around.

And also it turns out you are not the only mother-and-daughter showgirl team to have been in Vegas round the time you were first here. There have been at least fourteen mother-and-daughter teams! That I know of! That the super nice gentleman who is looking into things for me found. And *Jubilee!* wasn't a show when you were here the first time, so that was a bust. But I did learn that there are now six pairs of mothers and daughters currently performing. Twelve women. Four of whom are from Europe, and one woman is from Korea (but her daughter is American), five of whom have been saved.

Not by me. I am not here for saving anybody and it's maybe the kind of place where your own quiet example is a better alternative—where it is better to keep quiet about what you believe. (I don't, for example, know whether you do, either one of you. Or—if you do—what. Not even after the wonderful dinner last night for which this note is a Thank You, among other things.) This is not a place to feel alone about your beliefs: I see the billboards reminding you that God sees what happens in Vegas. There are people for whom the world is just preparation for what lies ahead, and so if you think I'd be up in arms, if you think I'd be upset, you would be wrong. For all that we do—however misguided—we are all of us in this world, and of this world, with its requisite portions of kindness and grace and kinship. And so I have been to a casino. I drank a margarita! I have watched people do things they will probably regret. Or that any rate won't make them as happy as they hope they will. What they have is my sympathy.

Listen: I am keeping those catalogs with all the naked ladies. I pick one up at every corner. I keep picking them up, I can't help myself. At first I thought it was prurience, but it turns out it was only like 90% prurience plus something else—less Song of Songs and no Jeremiah at all and maybe mostly just wondering what happened. Why so many? How do you end up where they end up? Do their folks know? Are they worried? Are there tense phone calls, tearful pleas to return, all is forgiven?

Mostly I look at them and just try to figure out what they're thinking. Last night, after I got home and fell asleep, I dreamed that you had pasted cartoon thought bubbles above the heads of all the girls on the catalogs. You knew what they were thinking. You wanted to let me know. One of the girls was thinking, I often dream of trains. Another, I am a lonesome fugitive.

I ask the girls in the catalog what I wanted to ask you last night, and I flip to the last page for the answer, but the thought bubble is blank. I'm about to fill in the right answer myself with a pen. (It is allowed. In the dream, with its dream-logic, what I write will be the right answer.) That's when I wake to sirens, friendly banter, and the mercy of temperate air in the dead of a Las Vegas night.

What I wanted to ask them was this: Are you really my mother? Are you really my grandmother?

★ ★ ★

Because the story we have is not complete. I know you left. You left and you said you were never coming back, didn't say a word when Uncle Carolina asked, "Well, what about the baby? What about the baby, Maryanne?" Then your mother, my grandmother, followed suit, though her plan originally was to come and get you back to Dade City, which apparently for all its charms and the heavy honey scent that hangs in the air from all the orange blossoms was not enough. Uncle Carolina says, No wonder, the two of you too beautiful and too much trouble for a town that small, always dreaming of somewhere else, always wanting something more—and Ybor City and downtown Tampa were never enough. You sent that photo—the two of you living it up, showgirls in the green-room, resplendent in pearls and youth. That was all, that's all any us heard from you, what you wrote down on the back of the photo: Having a wonderful time, wish you were here.

Though technically the second part was suspect. You did not wish we were there. Because there was no return address, no return.

If you are not who I hope you are, thank you anyway—thank you for the dinner and for not minding Hodge and for being so gracious to a stranger who kept asking you questions about showgirls and about your age and about your possible ties to Florida. I know I should have just come out and asked. I think you would have not have minded, would have told me for sure one way or the other.

There is this fear I had, before getting on the plane, before being assured by Southwest about Hodge and the pet carrier and being able to carry him with, that Vegas would be hostile. That I would stand out. That people would know that I was not here for what people are usually here for, and that they would be weirded out by someone who doesn't drive and takes the bus all the time and gets sweaty when he has to talk to people. Who doesn't talk much. Who at forty hasn't met anyone to be his special lady and maybe probably won't. Who spends most of the time he's not working at the pet shop playing *World of Warcraft* and *Everquest*. Who goes to church more than most people go to church.

But it turns out your town is full of kindness. Proof: I got on the 202 to get to your house and the driver said, "No animals allowed," and then he must have seen my face.

Who knows what he saw? I see myself in the mirror and I wince, but I have never not winced, not since I was a teenager. It is not a face to which kindness is naturally disposed. But the bus driver saw my face, and he saw me holding Hodge, and he nudged toward the back, and I deposited the $2.00 in exact fare, because I had looked it up on the CAT website, and he said that Hodge was cute. I told him that he was well behaved, that he wouldn't cause any trouble, that he was a very special animal. And he shrugged as if to say, We'll see. But he was smiling. Hodge was well behaved, as he always is.

I am sorry about the lie. I am not a reporter.

I know I had a notebook, and that I was taking notes, but I couldn't figure out how else to talk to you and ask you if you were my folks. And even then I guess it was harder than I originally thought, figuring how to come out and say it.

Like, in my mind, I was thinking I'd ask, As showgirls, is it necessary to sometimes leave the world you came from completely behind? Even if it means abandoning your home state and perhaps a small child? Does a life of adventure and glamour require an adventurous, glamorous person to cut off ties with those whom you (presumably) love?

But none of that came out. I have looked over what I wrote down on the notebook. The wrong things were asked. You were beyond gracious.

Had it not been for the notes I would have not realized how wonderful you were about my bringing Hodge. It had not dawned on me to ask if you were allergic, if you minded cats, but the both of you went right up to him and rubbed his belly and said that you had never seen a cat that was all right with having his belly rubbed.

And, still rubbing Hodge's belly, you pointed at yourself and said, "Anne Marie," and you pointed at your mother and said, "Anastasia," and you held out your hand in a jokey way but Hodge, being Hodge, shook it. He put his paw on your hand.

You also could not get over him being on a leash: "Look at him, just standing there! Like a little gentleman, so well behaved." And he was! With his big kitten eyes, his big *aggrieved* kitten eyes and his bright pink muzzle and his gray-and-white fur. I am not kidding about the eyes: Hodge always looks like some sort of pitiful street urchin who has been denied gruel, even though he gets fed this super fancy, super expensive boutique food I get with my manager's discount.

I said, "He is a very special cat." I asked if he could roam, and you petted him and said, "Of course," and we all went to the living room. All the while I told myself, Ask. Just ask. If you ask they will tell you.

Hodge, off leash, explored. I hoped to do the same.

But I didn't ask and I kept not asking. I didn't ask while we had the Chicken è la King, I didn't ask over the parfait. All I could talk about was the music: the one with the bright voice playing over a bouncy orchestra, then the one singing in a slow drawl, this low voice handling a Beatles song like it was a coal left to cool in a dying fire.

"Abbe Lane," you said, "Keely Smith."

"They played here," you said. "They played here all the time."

I have looked them up: a blonde and brunette, one with short hair and one with long. They belonged, the both of them, to a world I could never imagine and is no longer actually here: people flew in to Vegas in suits, they played Baccarat and listened to Abbe Lane while they had some fancy dessert. We eat our parfait. Abbe Lane sings *Mañana*. I ask about stage names. I keep thinking: Anne Marie, Maryanne. If you'd go to the trouble of changing your name, wouldn't you *change it* change it? Both of you are more Abbe Lane than Keely Smith.

I look at the photo in my wallet, the only photo I have of the two of you, then at the record covers, and what stops me from asking, finally, anything, is that it's not possible. If you are who I hope you are, you have not aged. So you are not.

You look *exactly* like the two women in the photograph. Not a day older. Therefore you cannot possibly be the women in the photograph.

I ask how long you've been here and the both of you make this sound, this concerted you-wouldn't-believe-it-if-we-told-you sound, and you smile. And it's the *same smile*. The same flash of teeth, the same eyes looking off to the side—that same sideways look that Susanna Hoffs has in the video for "Walk Like an Egyptian," to which I think, Man, I bet you think that's too loud. I bet you think the Bangles is too noisy. And it's on an oldies station! That's where they play the Bangles these days.

I asked what you did these days.

"We're retired," you said, and offered me coffee. You offered Hodge water.

"We miss it," you said, "but it's not the same. It's a tough life, a tough schedule, and it wears on you."

I don't know what I was expecting. I suppose there was a part of me that expected you to be like the crazy old ladies from *Hoarders*. A part of me was reasonable in expecting you to be old, which you are not at all: I kept thinking of the mystery and wonder of His creation. I wondered, Is this a miracle? But I also wondered, Is Uncle Carolina messing with me?

It had not dawned on me that the postcard he'd given me—the only documentation of my mother—could have been a fake. But it's not: He gave it to me decades ago, on my eleventh birthday, in an envelope next to the red-velvet cake shaped like R2D2. That was my present.

My mother, my grandmother.

Whom I had never seen. About whom I had heard all these wonderful stories.

I have not told you of the problems particular to being the unattractive offspring of a heartbreakingly attractive mother. People think you don't know, are not aware of your own ugliness, but that I suppose is a way for others to cope—the sense that maybe these people don't know any better. But I do. Not all the time, and not like it's this huge weight on me or anything. You do feel it once in while, though, like when you're sitting opposite two beautiful women, one of whom may have given birth to you—you feel it. You realize you don't bring joy to a room just by entering it. You don't, like the two of you do, light up the room just by virtue of smiling.

Someone at church told me that whenever she'd get mad at her parents she imagined that they weren't really her parents, that her real parents were these incredibly rich millionaires who had to gallivant off to some unknown rich-millionaire destination for purposes unknown, but that they'd be back and would free her from her these nightmare caretakers.

Uncle Carolina has always been kind to me, and though he's getting on in years he's still working the groves, still supervising the families that come in with the season. We talk every day. I never imagined him for less than he was and still is: a good man who took care of the farm and now wants me to take over. But I don't want to leave Orlando. I don't want to return to Dade City, with its minuscule downtown and where half the orange groves have been mowed down and turned into golf courses or subdivisions. I don't want to go back.

I asked you if you would ever go back, but we were thinking of different things.

You said that you couldn't really see yourselves in the outfits and the get-up anymore: the fur robes, the bobbed hair, the elaborate and sequined outfits, the feathered headdresses. All too heavy. And the hours were just too much.

You yawned. You offered me those hard red candies that only ladies much older than you keep around the house, and when I took one and thanked you for the very pleasant evening, you said, "I hope you liked Vegas. It's not for everyone."

And you said, "I hope you got what you needed."

The truth is that I did. The truth is that—I'm sorry, I shouldn't have done it—I peeked into your medicine cabinet, where there was a prescription for a Maryanne Carolina. It was not much of a mystery. I'm sorry. If I said I wanted to know, wanted confirmation, I suppose what I want, really, is for you to know that I have thought about you and loved you for as long as I have been alive. All I had was the photograph. I just wanted to see if you were real.

Soon I think I need to go back—back to Orlando and, not long after, back to Dade City. You don't need to write back if you don't want, and you don't have to answer the Craigslist ad where I ask about Lost Moms. You have been found. That is all. I'm just happy I had a chance to see you, and to talk to you, and to have you meet Hodge. I know that you cannot return. I know that you cannot leave Vegas because, whatever else, the both of you are happy here, even if so many others are not. The place has kept you young in its inexplicable mercy and its perpetual engine of hope—this whole place just runs on hope. I'm glad you're well here. I'm also glad I'm flying off soon: please write. I also wrote down my e-mail address. Do you have e-mail? Write however you can, whenever you can. Jim has promised that he'll forward anything to my Orlando address. And I'll be there for at least a couple more months. It would be wonderful to hear from you. I'll send you photos of Hodge. I keep a blog that is all just photos of Hodge.

You asked what I thought of your city, and you offered me a ride home, but I wanted to see what I could of the Strip before I had to fly home. Besides, it did not seem fair to have you drive so late in the night. The two of you looked so sleepy. You looked so indefatigable at first. And then so tired. It's this summer heat. It's this town stuffed with hope.

Listen: I have enclosed a copy of the photo. Here's the two of you forty years ago. They did it at the CVS—they'll take anything and they can duplicate it, so it's not a big deal. I just thought you'd like to have a copy if you didn't have one already. This is the photo I looked at when I was alone and though I had no one in the world, and this is also the photo that said to me, It's all right to travel. It's all right to go on an adventure. It's all right to see new things.

This is what I think of the city, what I think of when I think of the city. At the bus stop, after I left your house and me and Hodge waited to take the 108 to Tropicana, there was a gentleman who I am pretty sure was homeless—torn clothes piled on top of each other, two plastic bags brimming with newspapers, cans—and who had cut his knuckles badly. He had punched something, someone, who knows what. His hands were bright with blood. The skin around his knuckles had cracked and split and there were strips of tissue dangling. The wound was fresh but not so fresh so that the blood had finally settled, and into the mess of flesh the gentleman squeezed some Purell. He would squeeze the stuff in and then he would gasp and then he would keep doing it with the calm competence of a qualified practitioner.

We waited, Hodge and me. I didn't know if it'd be a good idea to offer help. I didn't know what sort of help I could offer.

And while we waited and the man squeezed the Purell into his wound we noticed a pigeon pecking at a Hydrox cookie. Hodge made his little pigeon noise—what he feels is a pitch-perfect pigeon imitation but is in fact a weird teeth-chattering non-pigeon sound—which the pigeon ignored. Two finches, each about a quarter the size of the pigeon, swooped in and took the cookie and moved it about a foot away. Hodge chirped at them too, to no avail. The pigeon pecked at the ground, found it cookieless, and waddled to where the finches were going after their loot, and he calmly, pigeonlike, continued to peck at the cookie. When the finches took it away again, the pigeon followed.

The bus arrived. The old man got on, and so did we, and we left the pigeon and the finches to their business. Look, my point about your city is this: The old man however horrific his wound found some sort of stopgap healing, and the pigeon recovered his cookie. The Budget Suites is full of cats, all kept safely indoors, all looking wistfully out from behind curtains, from behind miniature ceramic lighthouse collections and small plants. Hodge has not noticed his fellow cats, but I have. This is a place in which you need someone to be kind to. If any of the girls from the catalogs live here—and odds are one or two might, the one who often dreams of trains, the one who is a lonesome fugitive—then I bet they keep cats. I bet they take good care of them.

Domokun in Fremont

Iberia's mom's name is the prettiest name. Like don't even try, don't even pretend you could find a better name out there. Because you wouldn't. You wouldn't even come close.

Serafina.

It's a good name to say when you're going to bed and you've said good night and you've called your mom Mom, but then she's gone and in the darkness you need a sound to keep you safe. To keep you protected. You need a special sound.

Serafina, Serafina, Serafina.

It's also a good name to say if you're stuck in Fremont without your mom and left in charge of your two younger siblings.

Dad told them to stay seated on the bench because he had to help set up the protest, they had to see if the signs were high enough, if people would notice them, and you could, you could totally see them with the signs nailed to long pieces of plywood, the photos of the dead babies, these awful smudges of pink and red against black, like the flags of the worst country in the world. They had no babysitter, Dad couldn't afford a babysitter, but he couldn't afford not to be here, and they weren't supposed to move. But then they moved. Daniel took off and Iberia had to go chase him and Maria Lucia didn't want to be left behind. And so now they were like so lost.

Daniel's five and two months. Maria Lucia's thirteen months and one week. Iberia's seven but practically eight. Like a month and two weeks and a day from eight. So eight.

Daniel's holding her Domokun, which is not ideal but she needs both her hands to hold their hands. They're not supposed to let go of each other, not supposed to stray. And they know Dad's cell phone number, Daniel not so much, but she and Maria Lucia for sure. So she could find a safe grown-up and ask them to call. So she should do that. Because—officially?—she supposes that they are now very much lost.

Landmarks? She had like this map of landmarks in her head from the stuff she looked up in Google. From when her Dad said she was taking them to Fremont. Because she wanted to know, had never been, knew it was a Bad Place. Because that is all Dad talked about last month, Fremont as Ground Zero for sin, and so an opportunity. A place to testify. But now that they are walking it doesn't seem so bad, though she knows they should circle back, retrace their steps, find their way back to the grown-ups with the angry signs and the photos of dead children. Their spiritual brothers and sisters. Like the people Dad says they're trying to save. When you are in a labyrinth and you don't know where to turn you just take a right on every fork. She read that. But she's circled back already, circled too many times, and all the casinos look the same. Lots of light, lots of noise. Below the city of Las Vegas run vast tunnels through which stormwater churns and pumps elsewhere. She read that too. Sometimes homeless people die, get swept away, because they make their homes in the tunnels and the water gets them. The tunnels are like a labyrinth, a real one. In medieval cathedrals they set up labyrinths in the floor and you walked them and contemplated your salvation.

"Mom's not here, you know," Maria Lucia says. She jerks her hand, but Iberia jerks it harder. Doesn't let go. "Stop saying her name. Jeez."

Daniel says, "Jeez."

They should most definitely find a grown up. Somehow they crossed a crosswalk, which they were definitely *definitely* not supposed to do, and all around them is the press of legs in shorts and sneakers, and the noise is weird. It's all echoes and stumbles.

Daniel stumbles, falls on the sidewalk, Domokun on the cement. Which Iberia doesn't need her mom to tell her it's super dirty. Like, *Ich*. He's crying like he cries at home, with no sound, just the red face and the tears and the snot falling. Her poor baby brother. It's her fault, and she's in so much trouble, and she feels like it's taking her forever to get to him, to try to pick him up, to let him know that it's okay. Still running her mom's name in her head. Serafina. But also remembering the dream. The weird balloons streaming out of her mom. Domokun saying, I'm sorry, I'm so sorry. She wants to cry too, but Daniel's stopping, Daniel's smiling, so she can't. Because she's in charge, she's the one getting them where they need to go: to Dad, to the grown-ups. All the legs around them sweaty and heavy and moving fast. Even the motorized scooters zip by.

Domokun hovers in front of her. Floats. Wiggles a bit.

She's about to go Full Freak in public when she sees the arm holding her Domokun. Also the torn T-shirt, the scabs, the beard, the dirty face. A face dirtier than the sidewalk. Oh her mom would make her disinfect Domokun. Make her possibly give the monster up. The man says, "Yours?"

She nods. Now it's back in her hands, Domokun and all his new germ friends. All the millions of germs and bacteria. She holds a stuffed animal plus a new metropolis of microbes.

Which, fine. But her mom, in her head, she's the one having a Full Freak now, the Serafina she's been imagining for comfort is now freaking out, freaking out for reals. Like, I didn't raise you to pick stuff up off the street. Like, I didn't raise you to talk to people who live on the street.

Daniel's hiding behind her. So is Maria Lucia.

When you are lost you find a safe stranger and you have them help you find your parents. This is not a safe stranger. Far from it. You can tell he drinks. He smells suspicious. He wears too many clothes even though it is too hot, even though it is late in a day in the middle of summer. Of the worst of summer.

But the man's not sweating, and the man's not coming closer, and he's not doing the weird crouch-and-lean grown-ups do when they want to be all friendly. He's actually walking away. Like, actually leaving three children in the middle of Ground Zero for sin. And she—is she?—she is like saying "Excuse me?" like her mom says "Excuse me?" Which is to say not asking to be excused at all, *at all*. And so they're walking behind him, Iberia in front and her siblings behind, the man not turning, but not walking fast either. She says, "Excuse me?" The man acts like he doesn't hear her, like his suspicious smell shields him from sound.

She grabs his T-shirt. Also a metropolis for germs and microbes, she's sure. She grabs it and the man like tries to, thinks of trying to, pull away. When he turns what she sees in his eyes is awful. The man is afraid of her. The man is looking at her like she could beat him up, or like she could tear him to pieces. Like she's one of those tiny wolves going after a polar bear on *Planet Earth*. He's shaking. His hands jerk up, palms facing her. Tears in his eyes, his eyes red.

"I'm sorry," he says. "I'm so sorry."

"Excuse me?" she says. "We're lost? Our Dad's by the Hotel Alicia? It is cattycorner to El Cortez. It is two-point-five blocks from Glitter Gulch."

The man stares at her like he knows her. "I have to go."

"Excuse me?" she says. "You're a grown-up. You have to help."

He nods but he also says, "I'm not supposed to be here."

Maria Lucia says, "Please help us find our daddy." And Daniel cries. And Maria Lucia stands there thinking, my mom's the best mom, and if he even thinks of not helping us he'll be so sorry. She'll go full-on "Excuse me?" on him. She'll chase him down Fremont. She'll hound him. She sets her eyes on him, goes tough, imagines herself a full-size Domokun. A wolf.

He says, "Let me see your palms." They show them to him. She has to wedge Domokun under her pit, but he's suffered worse today. The man nods. Like, okay. "Golden Nugget. El Cortez. Okay."

The four of them huddle, all holding hands, Iberia holding the suspicious stranger's hand, though her mom wouldn't like it, and though Iberia doesn't like it, and though the stranger himself isn't such a big fan of the idea either. They walk slow. She thinks, Maybe the man could pick up Daniel, but she doesn't suggest it. Already it is a great kindness, this man who doesn't know them, doesn't want to take them where they need to go. Why push it? They walk slow, but there's no rush. The days run long. They are probably closer than they think.

The man says, "Nutters out there."

The signs. The blood and the babies and the words and the scriptures, all high up. This is just a practice run, Dad said. Just so we know how many people we can fit in. Just so we know if we can make an impact. The legs and the signs cluster on the eastern side of the street. The bench where they were supposed to stay put is empty still. A crowd that has nothing to do with any of them is hard at work watching someone spray-paint the Vegas skyline on a ceramic plate. The person dots stars and constellations over the Stratosphere. The crowd applauds. The heat is awful. She wants water.

She doesn't say, That's my dad. That's my dad you're calling a nutter. But she doesn't say thank you either. She says, "That's our bench! That's where we're supposed to wait, mister."

"Call me Merit."

"Iberia Sampang," she says, proud of her full name.

"Merit Stephens. Nice meeting you. Be careful. Be very careful."

Somewhere in the crowd of nutters her dad waves a sign, shouts a command, tries to get people to listen. They are not nutters. They are trying to do something good. They are trying to get people to think about what they do. Merit has let go of her hand. Merit very much wants to leave this place. He looks like he's saying, Are we done now? Like when you're dragged to a grown-up party and it takes forever and then Dad says, We're leaving, but they don't. They linger by the door and talk talk talk for like another hour. She wants to say, What's wrong? But she knows she can't. She knows that too much is wrong. Life is hard if you are a Merit. She's hugging him before she knows she's hugging him, before he has any time to think or say anything, so all he's doing is hugging her back. He's asking her to be super careful, to watch herself and her siblings. That this is not a good place.

"Is that why you were afraid?" she asks, still pressed against him. His shirt smells bad but not super bad. Bearable.

"I had a dream and you were in it," he says. But then he says, "It wasn't you."

She thinks, I dream of Domokun, of Mom and Dad, places I've never been. Strange places. She doesn't know if she's ever dreamed of strangers. Maybe she has and she's forgotten.

He says again, "It wasn't you. It was someone who looked like you. Esther. You looked just like Esther."

Just then the crowd shifts its attention from the spray-painter to dancers. The crowd roars and claps. The dancers spin on cardboard like tops, like planets, like they will never stop spinning. Merit's gone. Dad's in the crowd but he'll be coming back, he'll never know they strayed, walked Fremont, had an adventure. They sit and watch the dancers, and Daniel stops crying, and Iberia thinks of her dead sister. Knowing all the while that's not the same Esther. Can't be the same Esther. She watches her dad's signs, the dead babies swaying against the lights and the giant television screen. No one else seems to be watching them. The dancers are still spinning. She sits, her siblings with her, feeling very safe and very uneasy. She clutches Domokun and does not cry.

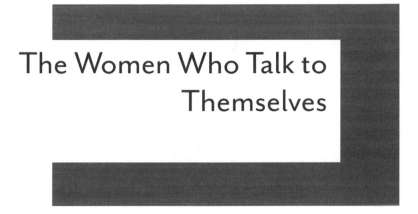

The Women Who Talk to Themselves

You would not think you'd fall for a woman who talks to herself, but there it is: It's done, it has happened. They are everywhere, and there are more of them this week than there were last week, and you have fallen for one.

And did you not think they were all squat or odd-looking? You did, and you were for the most part right. They wait on bus benches and point at random places in the ground as if signaling to low-flying birds or roustabout squirrels. They wear odd-fitting dresses. They are overweight most of the time. They are sad and slight sometimes. They carry strange items they have just purchased. They talk in high squeaky voices or low alarming murmurs. If there is another side to the conversation it is a side they are angry at or conspiring with, or it is God—like the short dumpy woman who thanked Jesus.

She said (three weeks ago), "Thank you, Jesus! My Jesus! I know my Jesus is Jesus! Thank you!" She carried a Publix bag with groceries and a cake and birthday items: candles, noisemakers, and party hats. And last week she was back on the bus. And she carried more birthday items and another cake.

And you suspected—and you are probably right—that these items are not really for a sane birthday party. That these were things she was buying for herself. Were you saddened by it? You were, a little—you imagined throwing a little birthday bash for yourself: no one else there, just you with a foil hat and a noisemaker, singing to yourself and making a wish. What makes it unspeakably sad is the effort. What makes it unspeakably sad is that it isn't sad, not for her, not really: that this birthday party is a true comfort, an honest source of joy, and that though you wish to sympathize you can only shudder a little—that your capacity for compassion and empathy is nowhere near where you would like it to be. You could not imagine anyone caring for one of these unfortunates.

You would not think it would happen but it did.

After nights of fitful work you take the bus to your apartment—to your cat, your beer, your TV. You drink and grow heavy. You have mown endless grass for hours and hours and your arms itch and your work clothes are stained with the juice of the field, and with burrs, and bugs, and bubble gum. You wake up tired and in deep need of morning shows targeted at women. You watch *The View*. Maybe, you think, you do not understand women. Maybe you are right. You watch *Oprah*. You are fascinated and perplexed. It has been a long time since you have had a girlfriend. Your shift begins at midnight—you are expected to be done with the grounds by eight in the morning. You are a short man and like all short men you have grown a beard. You own a cat that you talk to more than you should.

What matters is the physical. You learned this in high school. You learned that you were no prize. You learned that you could be sometimes charming and polite, and that charm and politeness helped a little, but not a lot. (And—you do not think about this too often and are vaguely reluctant to admit it—what matters for you is the physical as well.)

The woman wears a calico dress in the chill of this southern winter. She is tall and leggy and a brunette, and has very green eyes and looks vaguely Irish, and she is angular—she walks as though she was stabbing the ground, and did not want to; she tilts her head to inspect the ground and whatever she is saying is being said to nobody, or to nobody in particular, or to somebody who is not there. (You do not know why you are surprised by her beauty. You do not know why you find it odd that someone who has some kind of psychological problem could be beautiful. To your credit, you know that there is something wrong with that line of thinking, something ugly: You think of blind people in movies, and you cannot help but think that their real-life counterparts are not nearly as attractive, and then you remember the deaf girl with the golden locks and the honey skin in high school: how beautiful she was. But your compassion and your empathy—they are negligible.) The woman talks to herself, though you cannot hear what she is saying, she talks so low. And you are too shy and too struck by her beauty to sit closer. You avoid direct inspection. You would not think of approaching her.

She is lovely and you are in love with her, you think.

You think of what it would be like to talk to yourself like she does.

This is what it is like.

Tonight you step into pools of orange from the glow of the lamplights. You can see yourself and the lawnmower on the reflective walls of the low flat buildings of the research park. You need to talk a little louder—I can barely hear you—the lawnmower needs to be looked at once you get done with it. (It probably needs oil.) Have you wondered what they do in there, in those buildings? You have. Beats me.

What matters is the physical. What matters is that you are alone. What matters is that she is beautiful. What matters is that you will not reach her—she is not reachable, is not to be reached, is unreachable.

You think you can talk to yourself if there is no one else there. You do it for a few minutes before realizing that you cannot: It's exhausting and pointless. Your throat is sore. You wouldn't be able to do it all day—you would have nothing left to say in very little time.

If you stop right now this is what you will hear: the grumbling of the lawnmower, the Doppler decay of a lone automobile on the interstate, the hum of the electrical transformer by the building nearest you, your keys rattling in your pocket, the beating of your heart low and steady in your ear.

OK. Yes.

Yes, that is what I want to hear.

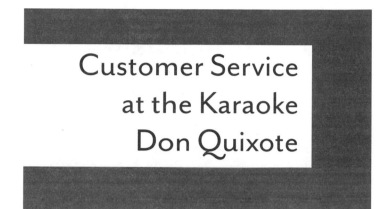

Customer Service at the Karaoke Don Quixote

Customer service at the Karaoke Don Quixote is main thing we worry about. Because if customer doesn't go here, will go elsewhere, and soon no customers go here period. We treat them special. We feign bad foreign accent to make feel better. We not decide on particular region—because if customer is from said particular region, or customer's family is, is no good, no? No. Is no good. Is little Italian, little Polish, little bit here and there. Is good.

Because it gets customer singing. Customer service is number one priority for us. We say, You sing, you sing! Is person drinking? Yes! Is good, for beer and spirits make person sing, and people singing is good: They buy more beer and spirits. And intoxication is good because is no cover charge. Is good, because people like singing great works of literature, and is good because they drink more, so more profits.

First we start with *Don Quixote.* But soon we branch to postmodernist stuff, because customers want, and customers is always accurate: They say, Barth! Barthelme! Pynchon! Coover! We say, OK. We say, is good. Also postmodernists drink. Minimalists, they don't drink so much. Is poetry good? No, is no good. Poetry karaoke, is like haiku, sonatinas—no good, no one sings. Classic is good: Melville and Tolstoy and some other peoples—big hits, big big hits.

Is reason for accent? Is annoying you? Logic? Logic is, these are shy peoples—literature peoples is shy. Is sitting around reading, no much dancing, maybe some drinking and then dancing, but stiff, you know? Is people reading travel, you know? The *New York Times* travel section? Also travelogues and such. Is dreaming of going elsewhere, maybe finding charming out-of-the-way spots with kindly innkeepers, lovely foreign women, also big motherly types that feed them exotic soups and ales and such. And maybe, in this fantasy of going places, they're thinking they might let go a little because no one knows them, right? So we feed that fantasy a little. Is good, is people happy. Is good business. People sing: They sing *Quixote:*

«En un lugar de la Mancha, de cuyo nombre no quiero acordarme, no ha mucho tiempo que vivía un hidalgo de los de lanza en astillero, adarga antigua, rocín flaco y galgo corredor.»

Or sing dubbed international public domain version:

"In a village of La Mancha, the name of which I have no desire to call to mind, there lived not long since one of those gentlemen that keep a lance in the lance-rack, an old buckler, a lean hack, and a greyhound for coursing."

Is good! Business is good. We have many franchises. As for matter of customer service—customers happy, is always happy here—service-wise we are number one. Soon we open in La Mancha—is ironic, no? Waiters feign heavy American accent. Talk loud. Slow. Is good. People feel OK singing. Is happy.

Soon: IPO. T-shirts. Website. CDs. Is good!

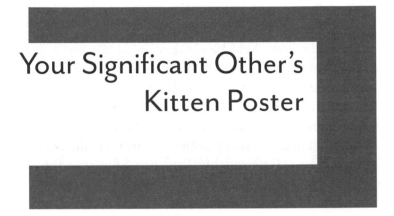

Your Significant Other's Kitten Poster

If the poster depicts kittens in a lavatory, smoking kitten-sized cigarettes, wearing kitten-sized British schoolboy uniforms, your significant other is a vixen and an outlaw at heart, and likely to run off with the first Hell's Angels biker to storm the neighborhood bar. The biker will break a cue pool on your back. Your significant other will light a cigarette and, her eyes clouded by passion, ride off.

You will be left alone. People will point and laugh. You will never show your face at the neighborhood bar again, which was an Applebee's and is now a Houlihan's—under new management, new posters on the wall, none depicting felines, but no matter, you won't go. You'll stay at home and grow bitter. You will resent bikers. Also cats.

If the poster depicts a kitten yawning in a kitten-sized hammock, your significant other is a nurturer. She wants children, or at the very least a kitten. She wants something tiny and furry despite all the intense conversations you had about not really wanting to bring a child into this world given the over-population and the sense that people stopped being totally themselves after kids—you talked long into the night at the café/video store, held hands, her ankle pressed against yours under the table. You said that if you had a child you'd send him to military school as soon as he was born. The kitten on the kitten-sized hammock reminds her of her younger brother, who does not resemble a cat in any way. She would not like a child that in any way resembles her brother. She does not actu-ally want a child, probably. But she wants a cat for sure. It's a shame you are allergic.

If the poster depicts a drawing of a cat by B. Kliban, your sig-nificant other is pure of heart and also capable of small feats of genuine magic (levitation, mind-reading, alchemy). She is waiting for the right time to tell you.

If the poster depicts two tiger cubs frolicking in a green field, your significant other is not so much into kittens as she is into wildlife. You have nothing to worry about. Except maybe *Gates of Heaven,* which you have not yet returned to the video store—it's been a year now, but you can't bring yourself to do it. You have kept the video as a memento of your first date. We are talking monster late fees. But you are not too worried ,and, besides, you are in love.

If the poster depicts a drawing of a cat in squiggly lines, your significant other is probably thinking of going back to gradu-ate school, where she will meet a professor that she will talk about constantly until, in a fit of jealous rage, you confront him. The professor will break a cue pool on your back. Your significant other will light a cigarette and, eyes clouded by passion, ride off on the professor's Harley. You will never go back to that Pierre Bourdieu book you were meaning to finish.

If the poster depicts a kitten hanging from a branch, your significant other is a secretary. She will file your papers and fold your clothes in ways that are both efficient and inexplicably irritating. You will be very happy and in love and have many children, most of which will serve illustrious careers in the military. You will sometimes weep when you are alone and watching the History channel. Hang in there.

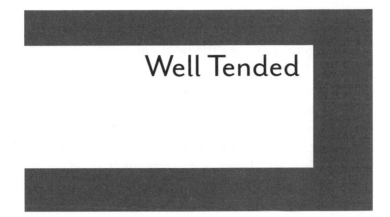

Well Tended

Because you moved, because my parents are out of town, and because any time I think of you my mouth dries up, is why I'm writing. Also: because I was going to tell you anyway. Because my mouth dried up right when you opened your door, keys in your hand, you saying "Hey, neighbor. Hey, cutie pie." You took a drag off your cigarette, and before I got around to saying what needed to be said—it'd been on my mind all day, all week—you told me that you were going away, did not know for how long, so could I watch the plants.

The manager said they'll be clearing up your place in four days. She said you're not coming back. I asked her how come, how did she know, had you written.

The summer's been too long, too full of afternoons where one judge show rolls after the other. I've watched them all. The one with the man holding a bat. The one where Kato Kaelin's the bailiff. The one where the judge always cries. The one where she shakes her head and her finger the same like they were windshield wipers. The one where he's black and grew up in a tough neighborhood and got in trouble with the law but now he's all right and wants to give kids in trouble a second chance.

Our neighborhood's fine: no sirens, nothing much happening, plus we've got the pool and the workout room, plus the park by the retention pond, the library and the Publix just down the way. Plus, you know, for a while, it had you. And now it's not just you gone, the whole place is a void. Kids flown north to see their dads in New Jersey. People working jobs or trudging through summer school, everyone my age clustered around basketball courts, basketballs, talking to girls like it wasn't the most monumental mystery, which it is. Everyone's gone. Mom's back in Colombia visiting the grandparents. Dad's near but sleeping mostly in the yard he rents in Bithlo. When he stops in he's got Acme beef jerky and *carrilera* tapes. I've daydreamed about this kind of summer all through last year, all through chem, all through gym—no parents, no one telling me what to do, nothing needing doing, some mysterious beautiful woman living right next door.

Because you had that smile. And that dark red hair and the blue eyes, which were too blue and too clear. And because for a white girl you tanned with grace. And because I can't believe you're fifty-three, not even when you said it and laughed and I asked you again and you pulled out your driver's license.

The apartment's clean. Your plants are fine, mostly.

I come in every day. I follow the instructions you wrote on the inside of the Parliament carton, though if I had had a moment—if I could have spoken—I would have warned you that our whole family has a tragic and like transcontinental problem with plants, mostly in that none of us can take care of them. Here's evidence: our father planted a sapling right outside the back of the complex, no branches, no leaves, just a gnarled palm-length of wood, which he tended all spring. The vegetation around it bloomed. The bit of wood refused to become anything but. One day we walked out to find that a leaf and a bud sprung out of nowhere, a speck of green and a dot of neon yellow. He was so excited that he ran back in the house, returned with a glass of water, poured it, and the little leaf and the bud fell right off, and that was that: back to square one.

I'm careful. Your directions are being followed, all of them, so I never give the ones in the living room more than half a tablespoon of water, always with the measuring cup you left on the counter, and I always mix in the yellow powder supplements, and I never ever hum or sing to myself or talk to the plants at all.

The whole time I'm there I'm silent. Shoes off. Curtains open. I do not put on music or turn on the television, and if I hear anything—or think I hear anything—I go by what you wrote and don't respond or nod or shake my head.

For the longest time I didn't know any of the other neighbors, but the problem with a long summer with little to do is that the world forces you to cluster around your own kind. That was how I ended up talking to Tulane last week, on our mutual treks from the Publix plaza, him back from the hobby shop with a model kit of a *Battlestar Galactica* ship and long clean planes of balsa wood, me with the Little Debbies and the bag full of library mangas, thumbed copies of *Neon Genesis Evangelion* and *Nausicaa* I'd already checked out at least twice before, plus the Hawthorne I promised you I'd read, as well as two books I knew nothing about but whose covers I loved: one a blurred photograph of clouds, the other a painting of a woman leaning from a balcony overlooking an empty city at dusk.

Tulane knew the shortcut from the park through the scrub to the back of our apartment complex. We talked sci-fi for a while, then shows. He has cable so his options are way better, but apparently he too had been getting to that point where it was all just too much, where even the idea of turning on the TV oppressed him a little—like it had switched from being a break to this duty, this job, this thing you'd put off as long as possible. He said he'd learned to regiment. Wake up at a certain time. Do certain things.

"I tend plants," I said. "I'm helping my friend. She's away for a while so I'm taking care of her place." There's a thrill—the same kind of back-of-the-neck joy you get when just about to dive into cold water on hot afternoons—in saying "my friend," in saying "she."

He said that you reach a certain age and you learn to appreciate the beauty of simple rituals. That you can actually spend a lot of time doing something in solitude and quiet and that you realize it's way better than anything you could have spent any amount of money on. He learned this early on, he said, in his twenties, and now that he's in his forties he's grown more and more grateful for it. He said that he's learned to love oatmeal more than he's ever willing to admit.

I tell him I'm Colombian and he tells me that so is his girlfriend, Lucia Inéz. I want to tell him what it feels like, sometimes, which is that everyone's Colombian, that the whole country's moving here. Sometimes, of course, it's the opposite: you feel like you're pretty much the only one. I'm about to say it but he's telling me about what he does for a living, so I keep quiet and listen.

He works mornings building miniatures of famous landmarks, which he sells on eBay and also at flea markets. He also works on commission. He'll be asked to do these incredibly detailed dioramas of people's houses and work spaces. The big sellers are office interiors, little gifts of appreciation for administrative assistants and corporate clients where the biggest draw is that it was all handmade, the models always accompanied by an index card detailing the methods, the materials, and the time spent, all of it handwritten in a careful script. He does these in the morning with a stopwatch and a journal where he records everything.

Lucia Inéz works a crazy schedule because she's pursuing a Master's in Daytona, so she can only visit on Tuesdays. On other days, when he's done working and there's nothing to read and nothing to watch, he'll build miniatures of our neighborhood: our Eckerd's (now a CVS), our library, our Publix plaza, the intersection of Colonial and Alafaya.

He's constructed other parts of Florida as well: an orange grove in Dade City, the inside of the Kennedy Space Center lobby, about half of Disneyworld's Tomorrowland and most of Main Street. Eventually he hopes to fill in all of International Drive—he's already completed the Ripley's Believe It or Not and the Wet 'n Wild—though it's our neighborhood that draws me in the most. I ask if I can see it. He says that I'm invited to dinner tomorrow, and that it'll be good because his girlfriend will be happy to see a fellow Colombian.

"She'll be happy to know I've made a friend," he adds. "She's worries I spend too much time alone."

We go to our respective apartments. I sit with the TV off, read the Hawthorne for a while. I try to imagine where you might be, the sun just about to go down, you with your red hair and brown shoulders out in Tampa or Pensacola, driving down I-95 with the palms and the scrub and the lakes all whipping past your driver's-side window like they've got somewhere they need to be right away.

In three days they'll be clearing your place. The manager sees me with your key by your door, tells me that I better not take anything, then she climbs back into her golf cart and crosses the half-block to the rental office. There are all these people I want to ask questions of, but they leave before I can get the words out of my head and into the world. Like, is someone coming in with a U-Haul? A Pod? We're second-floor people, you and I. There'll be a lot of lugging. Do you have friends coming in to carry out your books, your clothes, the unlabeled jars of bright-blue iridescent liquid in your fridge?

I open the door and reread the instructions and admire your handwriting. Its neatness. Its nearly perfect run through the cardboard, all straight lines, nothing out of place, no strike-outs, nothing messy at all. Had you been here I would have told you that what I like most about your writing is exactly like what first drew me in about you, the day you unlocked your door while holding two full Whole Foods bags, keys in hand, mail in your teeth: your grace.

I draw the blinds, go through the plants. I tear out two paper towels and dust your living room, though I'm pretty sure it doesn't matter, you're not coming back, you'll see no evidence of it, and I'm not particularly anti-dust. I like things tidy but I don't really dust our own apartment. Something in me—or not: not in me, something in your apartment—tells me that you'd like it that way, that the plants too prefer the place as clean as possible. Dinner's in half an hour, and while Tulane's models will most likely be wonderful and fine and odd, there's also the sense that the expectation will trump the experience itself. You told me much the same thing. I asked for a cigarette and you laughed and gave me one and said that I shouldn't light it. That the thought of a cigarette is actually for the most part better than the cigarette itself. That even when you've been smoking a while—that particularly when you've been smoking a while—what you're really excited about is the memory of the experience and less the experience itself: that it's a kind of nostalgia for something that has not happened.

You wouldn't take the cigarette back. You said to wait for when I'm ready for the real thing to supplant its idea. I still have it—I keep it in my pocket and one day when no one's around, when there's nothing to do, I will light it and smoke it and think of you, of what you said.

The apartment is clean, full of its usual murmurs and whispers, which again as per your instructions I ignore. And then I don't. The thick yellow light of the late Florida summer pours in, all orange blossom and honey, and the back of the apartment complex is dark and green with whatever remained of the afternoon storm, mute hairlines of lightning linking one cloud to another, the Alafaya traffic rolling unseen not too far off, and I stand very still in the middle of your living room and listen. You are elsewhere. Your cigarette is in my pocket. Your plants are talking to me.

"Where are you?" I say.

The room grows quiet. For a moment it feels as though an answer is coming—as though your voice would pour in through the roots and up the stem and trickle out of the leaves—but no one says anything, and it's as though my voice had broken off their chatter. They weren't talking to me. They were talking to each other. I wait some more and then it's time to go, and there's nothing to be done. I realize I'm being ignored. Then I realize I'm being ignored by plants.

So I blush. I leave the apartment. I lock the door. I stand right outside and wait for the plants to start talking again, though I'm now running a few minutes late and Tulane's unit is on the other side of the complex. I wait and wait: the conversation resumes, its cadence like rain bouncing off plywood and shopping carts.

Our Eckerd's has three newspaper stands, two bike racks, four handicapped parking spots, a drive-through window for prescription pickups, and five thumbtack-sized pigeons guarding its automated doors. The model has no windows, so you can look into the inside rows at the racks of shampoo and cosmetics, the center racks with their rows of discount shirts and Styrofoam coolers.

Lucia Inéz—tall, fair, freckled—leans in close and points to a miniature of herself examining two tubes of sunblock. By her side, near a stack of paperbacks, is a physics textbook and a tiny Colombian flag.

"They remind me of *chivas*," I say.

She smiles, walks to Tulane's bookshelf, and retrieves a *chiva:* a palm-sized, brightly painted clay model of a bus with a fanatically detailed interior. They sell these souvenirs all through Colombia. You go to any town, they'll sell multiple versions in multiple sizes.

"When I first met him," she says, "I'd just come back from Manizales. I'd gotten this but I didn't know who for." She tells me that she knew that she was going to give it to someone but didn't have anyone to give it to. That you go home and you're so happy to see everyone, it's like you never left. Then you come back. The principal had left her one of Tulane's models on her desk. Her classroom. It was all there, the rows of desks, the cubbyholes, the chalkboard, a red apple, the hamster cage. But there were no people. "Even the hamster was absent," she says. "Just the space."

Lucia Inéz puts the *chiva* back on the shelf. When she returns I am a little in love with her. I am a little in love with her partly because she is in love with Tulane. It's a problem. It's terrible to automatically fall for anyone who is nice to you. It is also terrible that I've missed some of what she's saying.

She's still talking about the model—that it was beautiful but so empty.

She puts her hand on Tulane's shoulder. She says, "That's when I knew who the *chiva* was for."

Tulane says that most clients still prefer the models to be empty, but he gives everyone the option now. He can put little people in there.

And he says that he had a hard time believing that the *chivas* were actual—as in actual buses that actually run through Colombia. But they do. They're everywhere, all conversions, with only the bus frame and engine remaining and the top handmade mostly of wood and strips of metal. They're painted green and yellow and red. The *chivas* connect distant rural towns. You can pile up as much as you want, all your possessions stacked high and precariously balanced, and you can ride on the roof and take all of it in, the steep curves and the chickens tied to the soldered knee-high guardrails and the bundles of grain and the boxes of stereo and computer equipment all secured with twine.

Lucia Inéz brought empanadas from the Colombian bakery. We eat those. We drink Pony Maltas. We have guava and cheese for dessert. I tell them about my dad's love affair with Mexican food: with how we've had nothing Colombian for like the last six months or so. It's either Mexican or beef jerky. And the music: how he's obsessed over *carrileras* since the convenience store by his yard started trying to get rid of its cassette section.

Tulane laughs. "What we want is always something else."

Which he's wrong about: they sit close together. They are so clearly *together,* so near each other. What they want is right there. I eat and say nothing and try hard to smile, to be pleasant, but can't. How does this form of contact happen? How does it keep happening? How can it keep happening?

"Always somewhere else," Lucia Inéz says. She adds that she had been teaching remedial science for the past two years, and had been daydreaming of doing the AP physics section, and now that she got her chance this year—big to-do at her school, one physics teacher dead of a heart attack and the other suspended, both events related, with even the local news covering the whole mess, had I seen it? (I had not)—she's happy but misses her remedial kids a little bit.

I'll be going into my sophomore year, but it's a different high school, and I'll be in AP history and English but none of the science classes. Lucia Inéz asks if my folks are proud of me and I shrug. Then I actually realize that they are proud of me. That I'm being a jerk for trying to pretend I'm this latchkey kid, this ignored kid who has been left to fend for himself this summer, whereas in fact it's all way more complicated than that, and also whereas I know—have been told—how happy I make them. So I correct myself: I tell them about dad's work with the cars in Bithlo, the effort to catalogue as many of the parts in the yard and put all of it on the website, and of mom taking care of her sister in Colombia.

Tulane asks if that's where the schoolbus races are. "Not Colombia," he says. "Bithlo."

I nod.

"Rednecks don't give him a hard time?" he asks.

Lucia Inéz says that her car broke down by one of the Bithlo convenience stores and that some of the nicest people in the world were the ones who helped her out that day, in that neighborhood. I say much the same thing: everyone's been wonderful. People have helped my dad out. There's all this software you can use to do inventory. They've helped him out with that, linked it to the Internet and everything.

Tulane doesn't seem convinced, but pretty soon we're talking about you—because apparently you didn't just make an impression on me. Lucia Inéz saw you around, doesn't believe me when I tell her your age. She doesn't believe me when I tell her you just left. She says that people don't just leave.

"She'll be back," she says.

★ ★ ★

I leave early because Tuesday's the only night they have together. I don't want to overstay my welcome. There's no one waiting at home, no one who'll worry, so I go into your apartment first. The plants quiet down when I open the door—it's not that late, close to nine, so I sit very still. I wait for an hour, but they won't talk. Who would? Who'd enjoy these interruptions? So I'm just about out again and this one lone ficus bursts with words, and they are all bright and melodious and cool. The ficus says *Hello,* says *Thank you,* says *Look at me!* I ask the plant about you, about where you are. I ask if you're all right. But all it really wants to talk about is soil, water, light. When I ask again, the ficus says, *Look at my leaves!* I ask for its name, and it responds with a long pure stream, all silver and glint and water—a brook, a river, the mercy of a public pool in the worst of summer.

I tell the plant good night, and all I hear, as I close your door, is *Look at my leaves!* That's all it says by way of good-bye as I walk away: *leaves leaves leaves.* It's just as well.

It'll be nice to go home and finish at least one manga and another Hawthorne story before I go to bed. When I close my eyes I see all of Orlando, all these round bright pools shimmering from very far up, all these lakes afire with reflected light. You're not coming back. You're well, and you're somewhere else, and you're not coming back. And you're never getting this. You'll never hear what I wanted to tell you—what I knew that I would want to tell you nearly from the moment I met you.

There's at least this: that I could anticipate this moment almost from the start. That I started missing you the moment you put your hand on my forearm that one time and smiled. That I try doing a little of the math—when would I have had to be born, or where, and where exactly would the two of us have had to have been. There's all these bits, all these eventualities, that would maybe have resulted in us being together a little while longer.

★ ★ ★

Your apartment is being cleared. It started in the morning, all these men coming in and hauling everything out, and when I go up to the manager's office and ask what's going on, didn't you have like two more days, she just shrugs. She says that I better not take anything. They don't put your stuff in boxes: they just haul it out and anything heavy just gets thrown off the top of the second-floor stairs and launched into the ground floor.

I run to Tulane's unit. He's working on a model of a bridge—it's a famous one, but I'm not sure if it's the Golden Gate or just one that's similar and elsewhere. He's painting it red when I knock. His brush is still in his hand. He's about to say something and I cut him off and tell him what's going on, and he says that he's pretty sure there's nothing we can do. Which I know. I know there's nothing we can do. It doesn't mean that we can't at the very least—I don't know.

He walks with me, then jogs along when I start jogging. They're still throwing your stuff—furniture rolls down the stairs and stays for the most part in only two or three pieces. I was expecting it to splinter, but it doesn't.

We dodge the debris, and the workers see us long enough to stop themselves from sliding a desk down the banister. Tulane asks them to stop for a moment, then he looks at his hand, which he's raised, and finds that he still has his brush in his hand. The manager approaches our unit in her golf cart.

It's only since meeting you I've been doing this kind of math, this trying to figure out where people fall age-wise, because before it was only like people my age and then, you know, *old*—but the manager must be a good ten, fifteen years younger than you, but she's old. She just looks old. And neither Tulane or Lucia Inéz or you do. Or—never mind—you do but you don't. I don't know how to say this.

The manager pulls up and asks what we're doing there.

Tulane's about to say something, but whatever it is will be too polite, too wishy-washy, and we'll get nowhere. We'll be asked to leave.

"She had some of my plants," I say. I don't usually lie. I don't like lying. "I just want them back."

The manager nods. "She was a bad tenant," she says. "She was too quiet, and she always acted like she was better than everyone. She had that attitude."

"Anyway," I say. "I just want my plants back."

"Because how could she. If you're living here you're no better than anyone."

We don't say anything, Tulane and I, and when the workers see that the ground is clear they let go of the desk. It lands with a terrible cracking sound, loud enough to resonate in your stomach. The desk actually splinters. It looks as though someone actually detonated it.

The manager says that I'm welcome to come in and get my plants. She tries to tell the workers, but they have a hard time understanding her, so she asks me to translate, which I do.

The plants are no longer there. There's two small piles of laundry, a mirror shaped like a crescent moon and one whose frame resembles the sun, and there's also four small wood boxes, all open and all empty. That's it. Everything else, I imagine, is on the ground, but the workers tell me that they hauled most of the lighter stuff to the Dumpster.

Someone ran the compactor. I ask Tulane to stand guard and make sure no one presses the button again and I go in, thinking all the while that it'd be a phenomenally stupid way to die. He was fourteen. He was trying to save some neighbor's plants.

I find them in pieces: soil, torn roots, leaves, all of it irretrievably mixed in with shards of CDs, rattan furniture, and actual garbage. I stand in the middle of the mess and try to listen and there's nothing. Just traffic. Tulane hasn't asked me why I'm so preoccupied with the plants, and I'm glad I don't have to explain. I just keep looking, I don't know for how long, but they're all too torn up to retrieve, no bit of the plants bigger than a knuckle.

Tulane's just outside the Dumpster. He makes a half-surprised animal noise. When I turn he's smiling and holding a foot-long ficus in a broken ceramic pot.

The plant's thriving, but it's not saying anything. Later that week the door rings and I answer and there's no one, just a package neatly wrapped in brown paper and twine. It's your apartment. Tulane left it unpainted and unfilled, so it's just this spare living space, and while it should be a little eerie or spooky, it isn't. It cheers me up. The note on the index card tells that it took four hours to build, and it also says that I'm invited for dinner next week.

That night, I hear the bright watery murmur again. The plant is confused at first, then happy, and then it tells me something I think I already knew but was afraid to even think about, which is that you hear them—that no matter where you are you know what your plants are saying and what they're hearing. What they're feeling. I'm not sure if the plant will pass along what I've got to say. I'm actually surprised, a little, at how indifferent the ficus is to what I tell it—like all it wants to do is talk talk talk and never listen—so I'm not sure it's passed along my message. I'm also writing it down. Because I have to. Because school starts soon. I'm going to have other things to juggle—the weight of other feelings and that strange underwater pull of desire, the memory of other eyes, other shoulders, other necks, other voices, and the strange and impossible magic of beautiful women, their grace and yours, and all of it rushing through, all of it so fast.

So I'm telling it to the plant and writing it down, but I'll say it again just in case. Because I know you're listening. Or because I hope you're listening. And because I mean it, and because, very soon, I am going to try very hard to forget you. That's all. That's all I wanted to say: I hope you're well, will always be well, you are too beautiful for words. I don't know why I didn't tell you that last time I saw you, why I didn't say I love you—didn't say Who are you, didn't say You are impossible and a miracle and what luck, what dumb luck, to live so close to you, to be so accidentally near you for however long. I don't know why I didn't. I don't know why I just kept saying hello.

Souvenirs from Ganymede

The snakes had nowhere to go, so they ended up in our homes. We extracted four from our A/C unit. They crawled in and wouldn't be found till the unit malfunctioned and stank up the house, and little drama was made of the extraction. We lived with live snakes and were okay with dead ones. The live ones ran through our gardens. A man with an unkempt beard was called upon to deal with those thought poisonous: He doused them in gasoline, lit them on fire, let them burn, and swung them into a ravine with a cartwheel motion. I must have watched that arc a few times. Mostly I remember the snakes found in the A/C unit—already dead, probably not at all that bright to begin with, sad, harmless.

They made their way to our ducts from 1979 to 1983. We lived in Guri, a worker's camp in Venezuela, on a low dimple adjoining what would become, when completed, one of the biggest dams in the world. Caterpillar trucks cleared the land in wide sweeps. The forests of Canaima burned, the smell sweet. We lived in paradise and were expelling the snakes.

The American and Canadian workers living in the camp took us aside. Showed us charts. Warned us about coral snakes.

Children chased coral snakes because they were small, hard to find, colorful, and had no desire to be caught. No one we knew was bit by a coral snake. Corals were shy, as were scorpions, which we sometimes found when we shook our sneakers before putting them on, although we put them on many times without shaking (we often forgot) and nothing happened.

Nothing happened with the arañas monas either. They were nothing more than particularly large tarantulas. They looked otherworldly, extraterrestrial, and they scattered out of unexpected places. Closets. Boxes. Pants pockets. Barbecue pits.

One scattered out hissing, on fire, out of the coals. It jumped out of the grill and onto a table and into the ground. It moved fast and passed right by me, a little alien on fire looking for a forest and finding nothing but pre-fabs and shrubbery.

Post-tarantula, Peruvian friends of my parents grilled anticuchos, marinated cow hearts, which I ate again only recently and which are better than you might think, specially if you don't know what they are before you eat them. The dish took me right back to Guri. These friends, Lucho and Lucia, also prepared exquisite fish seviches: chunks of raw fish marinated in lemon juice. Our Argentinean neighbors introduced me to mate and ark clams. People had flown from all parts of the world because Venezuela had struck oil and had too much money and didn't know what to do with it.

When they arrived in Guri, my father was twenty-five, a scholarship kid, an industrial engineer who turned down a Fulbright because he had just met the person who follows this dash—my mother was twenty-two, bright, a beauty who received a call from a former suitor on her honeymoon, the boy heartbroken and telling her that if she did not leave my father he would kill himself. She told him to go to hell. My mother was seventeen when she married, my father twenty.

They are extraordinarily good-looking people—toned, symmetrical, and (during their twenties, thirties, forties, and fifties) eerily ageless, young. They are in their sixties now and could pass for people in their early forties.

Their crowd in Guri was mostly young and unmarried. They spent their weekends on beaches, following long, artfully choreographed car trips.

I was the only child for a long time. When I visit my parents' friends or when they visit me, they tell me so, that I was this little thing chattering away with all the twentysomethings. They break out photo albums (they carry them on trips, and e-mail forgotten prints—what happened for them during their twenties never repeated itself, I don't think, never again that combination of oil-boom, disposable income, youth, free time; in sharing these photographs they are confirming an unlikely moment in the unlikeliest of places; they're looking for confirmation: Look, this happened, here's the proof; here's conclusive evidence). On those photos I'm at the forefront, flanked by limbs, dark girls in bright yellow bikinis, thin laughing men with sideburns and unbuttoned shirts printed with highly questionable patterns. They were into body-surfing, the waves on Playa Colorada peaking at twenty feet. They were all very young and full of a kind of energy whose afterglow I feel even now. There were bonfires. There were stops along the highway for coconut water, raw oysters shucked live and doused in lime and slurped down, and corn arepas topped with farmer's cheese.

There was the food, and there was also the sense of being unique among unique people—anything I said was listened to with more consideration than it deserved. We returned from these trips tired, sandy, and bronzed, soaked with and

overloaded by sun and waves, an intimation that what mattered could be drunk from the world in large draughts. I was
four, I was seven, and they all seemed wise, old, beautiful.

The dam dwarfed the camp. The Caterpillar trucks moved
chunks of earth on their backs, the diameter of their wheels
three times the size of a man. Cranes moved on steel tresses
along the concrete skirt of the structure. A detailed, scale-size
model had been built by the side—it used a small tributary
of the Caroní and replicated the larger structure in every way,
including fully functioning turbines that produced a trickle of
electricity.

I did not visit often, but did visit. The dam confirmed what
I already knew from watching Japanese cartoons on Venezuelan TV: *Capitán Centella* (*Gekko Kamen*), *Gaiking*, *Mazinger Z*
(*Tranzor Z*), and a few others that blended together. The world
buzzed with large and wonderful man-made structures. Some
battled crime. Others generated energy.

The camp itself was all pre-fab structures. It had two bowling
alleys, two country clubs, three cinemas, a handful of restaurants. There were large stretches of red dirt, dense clusters of
trees thick with the fog of rotting mangos, things half-built or
torn down or put up. Past a small mountain we found a cluster of houses made entirely of Styrofoam. Concrete would be
poured into them eventually. We tore chunks and moved into
hiding places and threw rocks at each other. We also threw the
Styrofoam, to no avail.

We often threw rocks at each other. We used chunks of clay
when we could but weren't very particular. These fights lasted
hours. Nobody won, and allegiances didn't last long, and they
were a lot of fun. A rock cracked my head and the wound

required a few stitches. We hurt each other all the time. We picked fights, chased dogs, raced bikes down steep ravines. The American and Canadian kids mostly stayed away. I befriended a few, partly because our Guyanan maid spoke English and I was learning and wanted to practice, mostly because they had the best toys. Peter had the Millennium Falcon and Slave One. He had an Atari. His grandmother mailed tapes from the U.S. We popped them in the Betamax and watched *The Smurfs, Rudolph the Red-Nosed Reindeer, G.I. Joe,* other shows, plus all those remarkable ads for cereals and action figures.

You got what you wanted in Guri. You asked for it and it was given to you. I was spoiled. We all were.

There was school. I don't remember much. I doodled on books, notebooks, any available surface. One teacher put me and another kid in a drawing class. The other kid drew fantastic, highly detailed cityscapes. They were intricate and full of technique and virtuosity: windows properly spaced, sophisticated instances of perspective, all betraying a reasonable sense of architectural theory for an eight-year-old. He drew UFOs hovering above these landscapes. They shot laser beams and set the buildings on fire. The destruction was in every level inferior to the city—the UFOs were crude, as were the lasers, as were the people on fire with their hands up in the air. But I remember the pleasure he got from destroying his creation. He always drew the city first in pencil, the devastation overlaid later with Crayolas.

When we drove at night my mom asked me to keep an eye out for a black cow. You'd only find it at night, a perfectly black cow that was a harbinger of something, I forget what. The roads in Guri were dark and, past the camp proper, unpaved:

long dusty strips amidst vast clearings. Bruised sky, small cones lighting a small patch of land, twin ribbons of pale earth unwinding into the car hood.

When I swam at night I was convinced that the squid from Disney's *20,000 Leagues Under the Sea* waited in the murky, chlorinated depths. Snakes, tarantulas, and scorpions didn't scare me—they were part of the landscape. But I'd only seen the giant squid in the movie and imagined it below me, as I imagined the shark from *Jaws* lunging from some unknown part of the pool. (Pete played the movie for me; he never let me forget that I ran out of the room about five minutes in, so that I didn't actually see the shark, but conflated the artwork of the movie poster with the music and the lurking camera— that was enough.)

At sea I swam and body-surfed in the smaller waves and poked dead grounded jellyfish with sticks. Crabs I didn't mess with: they too had an extraterrestrial quality. They could have been villains in any one of the Japanese shows.

Victoria was often kidnapped by these villains. I always rescued her. There was not much in the way of physical romance in these fantasies, but they were baroque, elaborate affairs.

Victoria lived three houses from me—she was Argentinean, two years older, spent time with me with bemused contempt and only if I agreed to play whatever she wanted to play, held my hand, informed me that we would be married when we grew up. She was light-skinned, blue-eyed, freckled, and has remained so. After Guri, we didn't hear from each other for five years, then she called: Her father had divorced and she was living with him in a houseboat docked in Caracas. The last time she wrote, she was living in another houseboat—Valladolid,

Argentina. She enclosed a photograph, asked if I remembered that we were engaged. She was still lovely. I would still rescue her from any Japanese robot that might come her way. I never wrote back and have not heard from her in years, so that she has remained fixed on a boat somewhere on the coast of South America, the first girl who ever took my hand, a castaway.

Ukio still writes to my mother. He could speak flawless Portuguese and a halting Spanish. He taught me chess and (he insists) Japanese, although I do not remember learning it, and if I did I've forgotten it all. I judged all of my parents' friends by the quality of their gifts. (Again: We were all very spoiled.) Ukio gave me some of my most memorable Matchbox cars, as well as my first LP (*Unmasked*, by Kiss) and a few decent Star Wars action figures. He has written to me a few times, and I try to respond but often don't, and there's a sense—with him and with all of these people, who I love and who make up a vivid part of my life—that in responding I'm mooring myself to that time, to those years that do not seem to have happened at all, and that in fixing any memory to the page, or to the screen, I am failing it, and failing these friends, all twenty, thirty years older than me, and failing to preserve it as it should be preserved. When we meet in person and talk, it's fine. We still do, from time to time. Ukio still looks very youthful. He's shy, and has flown to every continent, and has worked with several oil companies. He has never married. We all suspected that he had a crush on my mother, and on some of the other women of that group—he broke out the ubiquitous photo album, and presented me once again with all of us at an impossible time, an impossible place. They're all laughing. They're tanned and healthy, young, toned—they're all extraordinary people.

★ ★ ★

And there is, in remembering them, still a sense of having failed the actual, the memories. They're livid, effulgent, light-filled visions. Transcribe them and everything falls flat and leaden: They were here, we were all here, and now we are not. Again: failure.

I was three when I first arrived, nine when I left.

No one stayed in Guri. My parents and I left shortly before the Bolivar lost its value. The bottom fell out of the boom. Dad had converted our savings to dollars a few weeks before. We were packed and ready to go. Others did the same thing. Some lost all they had, Victoria's parents among them. We all scattered to distant places.

The first book I ever read for pleasure was read in Guri, and it was about a distant place. It claimed to be a nonfiction account of being taken aboard a UFO and flown to Ganymede. I don't know how old I was, or why I wasn't outside throwing a rock at another kid, but this book broke me in—I took it for truth and followed the author as he was abducted and shown a perfect civilization on a satellite of Jupiter. He warned doubters: It's true, I was there, it happened. I was no doubter. These UFOs could come in at any time, drop you in Ganymede. I finished the book and hid behind the couch, convinced that they were coming for me. I hid for hours.

There would be some comfort in failing to find any evidence of this book's existence. It should, like most of what I remember, betray some degree of doubt as to its existence.

It exists. Its author is Yosip Ibrahim. It's been translated to English: *I Visited Ganymede.*

I wish it'd been a better book, or that I would have seen that it was hoax, or that it wouldn't have affected me as much as it did, but no luck. The book has remained fixed in my mind. The terror of that afternoon is also fixed. Aliens were out to get me. What was written and printed was true. (And the aliens, by the way, were pretty benign folk, higher beings, quite evolved, so my terror is still perplexing. What was I afraid of?) Ibrahim's travelogue was lost in one of our moves, and I've never made an effort to find another copy, or to figure out who the strange man behind the very strange abduction story turned out to be. He is part of Guri. And Guri is gone.

The dam has been built. The last stage flooded our neighborhood. Our old pre-fab house lies beneath the waters of the Caroni river. I'd like to tell you that you can see the rooftops on sunny days. I'd be lying. I have no clue, but know that the water would in fact be shallow by where we lived. It is now smooth, crystalline, calm, probably pleasant. I've seen photographs. It looks pleasant enough. It doesn't look like anything I remember. They did not raze the neighborhood before flooding, so the houses are all there, and one could, in theory, revisit them: the wide garden, the built-in bookshelf where Ibrahim's book waited for me, the yard where our dogs and our one turtle played. One could dive. One could find concrete evidence.

The dam has been built, the house has been flooded, and that should be enough, but there is also this: my parents, in tennis whites, walking toward me. We're at one of Guri's two country clubs. My father has put his hand on my mother's shoulder. They're smiling. They're walking toward me.

We fail. Life is essentially a string of failures: We fail to stay in one place. We fail to be the people we'd like to be. We fail others, others fail us. We fail to live up to expectations. We fail to resurrect the past, or to let it go. In end, we fail to keep on living, which given how much practice we have at it, we should be able to keep at it forever, but don't.

My parents are walking toward me, are looking at me, and I'm convinced that I am loved, will always be loved, and that this love will never waver. This certainty has not been challenged. It has not changed. It should have. This love, like everything in life—which after all is given to swift turns, shapeless shapes, random bursts of grief and grace—should have failed. It hasn't. These are ancillary mysteries. They are peripheral to the business of living but crucial, because they keep us going. They're part of the mystery train, the threads tying us together, the ghosts of fingerprints: They are at the heart of beauty. They are light falling in certain rooms on certain mornings.

The Coca-Cola Executive
In the Zapatoca Outhouse

The Coca-Cola executive was kind to me, though everyone was being kind that summer—an automatic kindness, one that I never questioned at thirteen and wouldn't question now at thirty-three. We were at his office because he agreed to sponsor the envelopes on which my hand-drawn, machine-reproduced bills would be sold. The envelopes would be printed on red tissue paper with white lettering and the Coke logo to the side of the shield of my imaginary country, whose currency I began drawing obsessively after I was diagnosed with Duchenne muscular dystrophy. The diagnosis turned out wrong, but that is of no concern here—neither is the imaginary country.

I had been drawing my whole life, and my obsession turned to engraved matter: official seals, notary receipts, stamps, and money, particularly American dollars.

After I acquired some confidence in mimicking the whorls, the grooves, and the odd border lines surrounding the words in pesos and dollars, I created imaginary bills for an imaginary world populated exclusively by sharks and surfers. People at school bought originals and photocopies, traded them, made special requests. It was my mother's idea to mass-market them.

As for the disease, it turned out not to be MD but dermatomyositis, a less severe acquired muscle condition that, like MD, causes severe weakness and atrophy. It took a while to correct the diagnosis. There were several years of treatment, additional diagnostic exams, and a four-month period of being unable to climb stairs, swallow, or do much of anything.

The disease is never quite wholly cured; the chances for a flare-up fade over time. Unfortunately, years later, I am dealing with one such episode—you take corticosteroids, watch your weight balloon, your flesh growing taut and odd, rolls of fat ribboned atop each other till you become the Michelin Man. Your ass swells, and, when you eventually recover, you are left with pale violent stretch marks that scour your buttocks and thighs. You feel weak, you feel hormonal. You cry. You fall into fits of rage. Your mind wanders. You feel, no surprise, very sorry for yourself. You become so self-absorbed, your mind so consumed by the unfairness of your predicament, that it's hard to conceive of someone else's misfortune.

I had forgotten about the Coca-Cola executive until recently, when my uncle, visiting my parents in Texas, brought him up. The executive had nearly died last year, in 2005, when he had attended a reunion. The school was an internado—a year-long boarding school of last resort.

In the mid-fifties, the executive, then in his teens, had messed up. My uncle was vague on the details; he had been kicked out of schools; he may have gotten into too many fights or he may have simply neglected to do his work.

He was sent to the internado. Most closed down in the seventies. The three that remained, the executive's among them, were finally shut down in the mid-eighties, though the building had been preserved and was still owned by the church.

You stayed in the school year-round. The only people you knew were the people you lived with, the janitors who took care of the place, and the priests and teachers who taught and disciplined you.

These schools were built in remote, high pockets of Colombia—not all of them were run by priests. The internados had a mostly positive effect. Some children had been sent from other countries—Ecuador, Peru, Argentina—and, at least for this particular Zapatoca institution, whose reputation for handling the recalcitrant was at its zenith in the late forties and early fifties, from Sweden, which sent two moody, dark-haired children with dark intentions, who never bothered to learn Spanish and wouldn't smile, wouldn't learn, wouldn't play tag or fold paper airplanes with the other children, but who nonetheless showed up at the fifty-year reunion with twenty elephantine Ikea gift bags, each bag about the size of a Renault 9, a car that still zips and rattles through Colombia. I hesitated on including this detail, since it is too absurd, too hard to take in, but my uncle assures me that it's so, and that the twins arrived with a rented truck; many of the guests donated their gifts to the town, since they had never anticipated carrying anything that large through the small winding road that connects Zapatoca to the rest of Colombia.

The twins worked for Ikea. They were both—like many others at the reunion, like the blur at the heart of this story—executives.

The children had thrived. They had all gone on to business. They had all, unaccountably, pulled out of shiftlessness and into diligence. They had all earned MBAs.

The Coca-Cola executive returned to the Zapatoca internado with a dead arm. Three years before, he had driven himself and his family to La Mesa de Los Santos—he had a family, probably a kid close to college age and another one a bit younger, and odds were, if they were anything at all like the other kids at the Campestre, one child or the other was following in his father's footsteps and was up to no good, but of course there's no telling.

Still, a man with a steady job who doesn't gamble much, while playing golf, and a member of the club, likely had a family, so yes, we don't have much of a choice, let's give him one (this part is pure conjecture, but odds are it's close to the truth): Mariluz, the wife, is darker than him, slender and pretty; the oldest son, Ricardo, listens to early Pearl Jam and one or two Colombian death-metal bands and way more Pink Floyd than anybody should, and though he is dark like his father, with the same unfortunate belief that a moustache is okay, and though he has done his share of massive Colombian-style drinking, which involves shots of the clear, lethal, way-too-sweet aguardiente chased by orange soda, and though he wears those oversized black T-shirts with band names blazoned across the chest, he is getting his BA at el Externado in Bogota, and will go on to McGill in Canada, where my cousin Juan David will befriend him. About Martinica, the youngest, the less said the better.

They were driving from Bucaramanga to La Mesa. The drive takes thirty minutes, and it's one of the safest in the region, though the path is winding and steep, with no guardrails and giant blocks of pale orange rocks hanging directly overhead—one steady zip up a giant knuckle of the cordillera.

Kidnappings hardly ever occurred in La Mesa; there was some petty crime, a lot of bar fights, but nothing major—no killings, no guerillas. The place is heavily guarded. Drive up to the first tollbooth—three men with automatic weapons will check your cédula against a PeopleSoft database of known felons and guerillas and respectable citizens, and you will be let through. Access, in this rural spot of Santander, is heavily restricted.

There are two golf courses in La Mesa, and four country clubs have their actual "country" country clubs up there, and there are hundreds of fincas, country homes, scattered along the dirt roads. All is green and cold and crisp. On Fridays the farmers receive their paychecks and you see them in the poolrooms and the tienditas, and hours later you see some by the side of the road, passed out from beer and aguardiente. La Mesa has not changed—there's a bit more electricity, better access, the roads are smoother, but most are still dirt, and some attention has been given to preserving the clumps of forests and the wide fields.

The event happened late one Wednesday; the Coca-Cola executive was driving late at night, alone in his old Renault 6, the family left behind at their country house—a car that was still seen on the roads, but rarely: It was slowly fading, falling out favor after years of loyalty. It was also blowing up a lot. Semana reported that the Renault 6, easy to break into, was the target of choice for stealing and then leaving by some police station, stuffed with explosives; it is apparently tailor-made for car-bombs.

But apparently also confusing to the people who confronted the Coca-Cola executive. It happened like this: Earlier that afternoon, while still in Bucaramanga, down from the bustle of Cabecera, two men driving a Honda Civic followed the executive to a Conavi ATM. They tried to approach him but failed. The ATM camera shows them walking toward him, then away, two men scuttling offscreen, although it is hard to imagine them being intimidated by a moustachioed man in a polo shirt and jeans (thick belt, small cell phone clipped to it). Loss of nerves? A police officer or a private security guard might have passed, a heavy long-barreled weapon hanging from the shoulder. A little girl in a Jessica Simpson T-shirt might have chosen that particular moment to tap on the glass of the Civic. The Coca-Cola executive might have reached into his pocket. This last action is likely: He would do so later on that evening.

So the men followed the Renault into La Mesa. They were not flagged down at the retén, meaning they had not been caught or had not been doing this sort of thing at all, if ever, which my uncle says was likely, given how they acted.

The men are young and skittish. The Civic they're driving is not so much a stolen vehicle as one borrowed, more or less, from a friend to whom they will be returning it soon.

In the late afternoon, the smaller towns in the lower hills surrounding La Mesa turn on their streetlights, and the countryside becomes flat and black with the occasional scattering of white and yellow dots. La Mesa has fewer lights. For a long time no electricity was piped in and everyone depended on generators, so driving down the dark roads was hairy.

One saw little, and whatever was visible was also blurred and incandescent from its proximity to the headlights: eucalyptus and yerbabuena branches perpetually falling above you, never quite landing, the eyes of a cow or a horse or a dog suspended directly ahead then winking out, beams and barbed wire, bars lit bright, music blaring. Then nothing. Dirt and road and darkness. The situation has not improved much. You drive under the occasional glow of a streetlamp, but the road you drive on is still unpaved, long patches of it still unlit.

The Civic nudged the Renault to the side of the narrow road. The two vehicles, one jammed at an angle with the other, blocked all access. Anyone driving this patch of road ran the risk of running straight on into the men who were screaming at the executive and jumping up and down and getting too close to the Renault, so that one of them (it's still not clear who) broke the driver's-side window with the barrel of their gun. This last action was likely unintentional. They probably meant to get him out of the car, to show him that they were armed.

The executive climbed out of the car. The men, for reasons still unknown, stepped back. It was as though they weren't quite ready for this part of the plan—they knew they would pull him over, and they knew they would get him out of the vehicle, demand whatever money he had, which they were doing, loudly and with a squeak here and there and repeatedly, but they had not counted on the physicality required: they gave him room. He could maneuver if he wished.

He did not, of course, wish to maneuver. Although there are people who will resist, the Coca-Cola executive was not one of them. It wasn't a question of him being overly fatalistic. Instead, he knew that, given his position, he was a target; he had not thought he would ever be kidnapped, though the company did sometimes provide him and others with occasional protection if they thought it was warranted; this particular executive, however, had not appeared a likely target.

Which of course didn't mean he wasn't. In Colombia you went your way and lived your life—played your golf, raised your family—until something terrible happened to you or to someone you knew.

Take the woman, the wife of a cattle rancher, who drove her Range Rover through the llanos orientales, the wide open plains of the south-east—she rolled through the territory, notorious for its kidnappings and its pockets of guerillas and paramilitaries, with an Uzi hanging from her shoulder; she said that she would prefer not to be kidnapped, and to take a few of the criminals down herself; in the club, she wore pantsuits, a little too much makeup (a little too much makeup is the standard amount of makeup for most country-club women), and modest earrings.

My sister's first boyfriend turned himself in to the guerillas in exchange for his father, who had been in captivity, and sick, for four months. The father had heart trouble, compounded by a bullet wound from the kidnapping: He had been stopped, dragged out, tied, and hauled to the back of a pickup. The back had not been closed. He rolled out of the car, jumped out as best he could and, still tied, inched down the steep wild banks of the countryside. The guerillas eventually figured out he'd gone AWOL, backtracked, found him. They put him back in the pickup, pressed the gas but did not, God knows why, close the back again, so the man jumped out once more (these must have been hairy jumps, but he didn't break anything), and this time, because they were keeping a better eye on him, they managed to stop in time and chase him down. They fired a couple of warning shots, and one of them hit him in the leg.

It is a matter of perpetual amazement to all Colombians that some of the worst brutality is often accompanied by equally violent displays of incompetence. If one didn't kill you, the other could.

In the meantime, you lived as others do. That is how people go on. This mode of thinking is not, should not, be thought of as exclusively Colombian. Random terrible events can occur to everyone anywhere—it is the virtue and privilege of the human animal to be aware of this fact and to keep going, keep enjoying all there is to enjoy, including a drive, in one's Renault, in the cold dead night of La Mesa de Los Santos. The thieves asked for the executive's wallet.

The executive reached into his jacket pocket. The air was still and the moon shone through fog and clouds—the world was blue and white. The men panicked and shot him in the arm; neither had asked him to hold still, and neither had heard the executive say, over and over, to keep calm, to keep steady, that he had his wallet right here and that they should take everything.

They took the wallet and drove off. The executive, now bleeding, waited for a car to drive by. One did in fifteen minutes. It didn't stop. It made a halting attempt at stopping or slowing down, then accelerated, the executive all the while thinking, I would have done the same thing. Three more cars did so as well. Eventually, a Leche Alpina trucker stopped; the executive rode to an emergency hospital alongside a smallish cargo of Kumis, arequipe, parmesan cheese, and lactose-free yogurt.

The internado must have faded white walls and faded red brick, though the outside fence, while also built of bricks with broken bottles glued along the top, was a bright virgin blue. Even though Zapatoca is a small town, with little money, it has developed a reputation for civic pride in Santander. The whole town was freshly painted.

The school had been built in the forties. Red brick, highly ornate patterns on some walls. But also: tight and small and a box, with an outhouse a considerable distance away.

This outhouse—a rectangular building with four stalls, a long wood plank, and a deep trough that emptied into a pit some twenty meters away—had not changed since the alumni had left. The building had closed down twenty years ago. No one had ever bothered with inside plumbing. You walked a long, narrow, dirt path to the brick cubbyholes, and the walk was cold. Zapatoca was high up, two hours away from and a few hundred miles higher than Bucaramanga.

Most of the alumni stayed with relatives. Some at a hotel. A few, the Coca-Cola executive among them, chose to return to the school.

How old they must have looked to each other. The Coca-Cola executive must have looked particularly old: everyone at the club, my uncle among them, had commented on the dramatic effect of the robbery.

He had lost weight. He could not use his right arm. He was no longer, indeed, an active executive. The Coca-Cola company took care of him, and he received the pension and disability due to him, and on some days he stopped by the offices in Bucaramanga, though he had retired to Cali; he was a damaged beast, no longer good for whatever it is he was supposed to do, and he no longer showed any interest in golf or tennis.

He did look older. The others had also aged.

The talk stayed moored to the past. They treated it as though it had been a far more innocent time. The injured Coca-Cola executive was not the only victim of a violent crime; two fellow classmates had been kidnapped, another killed, four more robbed; all knew someone who had been kidnapped; most knew someone who had been killed. They did not talk about how Colombia was going to shit, because none of them believed it; they all liked Alvaro Uribe, whose presidency had marked a hard turn to the right, and they all seemed to think that things were actually getting better.

They could not account for half the class. Some had not been tracked down. Some refused to answer the invitation. Some could simply not make it and regretted it and let the rest know. Of the nineteen, only ten had returned to the internado fifty years later to see what time and the world did to recalcitrant children.

The world had treated them well. They had all done fine. They all knew it, and they all suspected that the internado might have played a part, though the part must have been obscure. Their reminiscences returned, again and again, to the breaking of the school rules, to getting away with drunkenness or disorder or laziness. Despite everything, despite the worst fears of their parents—some dead and all older than they could have imagined—here they were, back in the most remote moment of their existence, back to the most secret, most lonely episode of their early adolescence.

They talked for hours, drank a little or not at all, and at the end of the night, after having toured the old school—all still there, and though small not as small as they thought it would be; the memory of the space filled it out; the width and breadth of their isolation expanded its dormitory, its dining hall, and its two classrooms with the tiny portholes into the mountains far away—they retired to their hotels and host homes. Only the Coca-Cola executive and two others remained in the internado.

The executive looked well, considering. He had been ashen. Would not discuss the robbery attempt or what it felt like to be shot but did talk about his children and wife. How wonderful they had been after the event. How lucky he felt, considering. How one never knows what's going to happen, and how the country has gone to the dogs, and how a man's word is not worth what it used to be—that he remembered when all anyone needed to do business was one's word. You'd say you'd agreed to pay this or that and it was enough. But not any more.

He retired to an old bed in his old room. The bed was small, smaller than a twin, with a thin mattress and a thin blanket. He had brought his own wool blanket. His wife had packed light, but she included the thick peasant blanket because the executive remembered the thinness of the internado's bedding and the irrevocable cold of the place. He shuffled and reshuffled the blanket into place and wondered if it would take him long to fall asleep (he had been a light sleeper then, and the lightest cough or snore from a classmate would startle him awake) and as he was wondering he was gone and could not remember, later, what he dreamed of.

He awoke two hours later, his bladder full. It took him a moment to remember that the outhouse had not been moved; indoor plumbing had not been installed. He padded out in boxer shorts into the cold, down a twenty-meter dirt road no wider than his feet, and into one of the four narrow cubicles cut into the face of a mountain, each with a wooden door and no roof, so that one could squat and stare at the stars and feel the wind, the chill, the Andean brace of the night.

He locked himself in.

The door, heavy, swung hard and shut itself behind him. It would not open.

There are doors of this sort everywhere in Colombia.

So the executive shivered for a time, and knocked hard, and yelled, but no one could hear him over the wind. He realized that he was going to die of exposure—to die of cold—in thin clothing, in the school that had given him his start in life, his first big turnaround. He knocked again and tried kicking but no luck.

The moon etched itself nitid and bright against the dark. And the night grew colder.

How one comes to make a decision of this sort is largely a mystery, not because it's particularly difficult or emotional (given a choice between doing nothing, and dying, and doing something, suffering, and not dying), but because one has to resign oneself to pain right from the beginning. He took hold of the edge of the door by stretching his arm, the one that worked, and he jumped, one quick awful jump, enough to give the flex and his forward motion the necessary momentum, he hoped, to go over the wall.

He did not go over.

He knocked his face against the door and tried again.

An hour later, he succeeded.

The outhouse door had never been painted, or buffed, or sanded. As a student, he had often dreamed of escaping through it, but he had never, not really.

My uncle said that the executive was hurt—that the outhouse experience, which could have been an anecdote to tell over hot chocolate and eggs that morning, something to laugh about, required stitches, that his skin was badly torn, that some ligaments were damaged, that the working arm lost some of its mobility, that the face of the executive was practically unrecognizable from the bruises. The outhouse had been a worse experience than the botched robbery, the executive would say, not laughing at first, and later laughing but not really meaning it, wondering at the strange nature of Colombia, this impossible place he had been living in all his life, with its heavy doors that swung shut, with locks on the wrong side, so that transactions that would ordinarily not require much effort turned, without warning, into life-and-death struggles.

There's the executive, wondering and thinking back to his time in the internado, when he was young and Zapatoca was all he had, and he was happy, and thinking back to the homecoming night, 2005 and every continent ablaze with random misery, a man with a potbelly and a moustache, swinging and scraping against the door, full moon lighting this world, not knowing what was going to happen to him and immensely interested, fascinated by his own dilemma, and for all his pain, there was this much: swinging over that door—making it through, knowing that very soon his body would be in all sorts of pain, a free fall on the other side and nothing to stop you but your own head and one dead arm—that one clear moment where flight had been achieved, where liberation had occurred, about that moment he had no words and usually kept quiet. What could you say? He swung, landed bleeding, and lived.

Correspondences Between the Lower World and Old Men in Pinstripe Suits

Gustavo called as I was about to ring Renee's door; the phone chirped the first few bars of Leonard Cohen's "Suzanne." I would just as soon have a regular ring, but I set the phone to random depressing songs after a bad breakup and lost the software to set it back. I thought about the breakup more than I care to admit. It was gray and raining but patchy, with brief random sun bursts. Across the street, an orchestra of children played to an audience of grandparents—violins, a song belonging to the repertoire of my cell: Willie Nelson's "Blue Eyes Crying in the Rain."

I rang the doorbell, thumbed the green button on the phone, and talked to Gustavo while the slightly off-key violins clotted the background. He wanted to borrow one of our blue boxes, which we used to recover data from legacy systems. I said, Sure, no problem, and asked him why he needed it, but before he could answer, Renee answered the door.

"I'll call you back," I said, and hung up.

The children stopped singing. One perfect plane of light hit her corn-colored hair, then her dark forehead, then one of her eyes, then vanished. She tapped at the fold of skin near the eye, under the tear duct, as though brushing away a tear. She had been crying but was not doing so now. The brushing-motion remained, refused to let go.

"I'm sorry about your loss," I said.

"Come in," she said. She shook my hand and turned. We made our way to a dormant computer. I knew, from the call ticket, that Renee's father had passed away, and that, in an effort to remove evidence of an affair, he had deleted program and document files from his system. Renee wanted to recover the lost documents. "I don't know," she said, "but I think he would have said something in there. He was writing to her all the time."

"That must have been awkward," I said. "They worked together, right?"

"They taught high school," she said. "They really didn't see much of each other at work. I don't think they did. I don't know. I really don't know much. She doesn't want to talk about it."

"It must have been awkward."

"He wasn't a bad man," she said. "Nothing like a bad man. He was really mellow. He taught physics, for fuck's sake."

"Oh. No. I didn't mean to say he was bad," I said, "but the situation—any situation like that—it's not like he's bad. But it's awkward." I patted my orange jumpsuit, checking pockets for the sheaf of CD-ROMS, serial cables, USB connections. Most of it was unnecessary, but carrying it comforted me. If I were to ever need it, it was there.

The phone chirped again. Gustavo. Neil Young's "Unknown Legend." I turned it off before it reached the chorus, inserted a boot disk into Renee's father's computer, and turned it on.

Renee inspected the jumpsuit. The computer whirred to life. I had come across the same sort of look a few times before.

Not often. I was getting better at recognizing it—it didn't necessarily mean much: things would get rolling or they'd go nowhere, but I did not intend to press the matter one way or the other. I was here to do a job.

"You're from Colombia," I said. Her skin was fair but coffee-colored, and I was struck again by her hair: wiry and half corn colored, half rust. Her voice, too. But I suspect I'd have suspected regardless. Had I seen her from across the way, there would have been something: some sign, a subdermal hint. We find each other even when we don't want to—don't want to find, don't want to be found.

"You too," she said. "I mean, no. My parents are. Were. I'm from here."

"I'm not," I said.

Nor was my boss, a transplanted Chiquinreño entrepreneur who insisted I wear the orange jumpsuit and who is also responsible for the Humvee with the paintjob. I match my company car. On the hood of the car on the back of my jumpsuit is a line drawing of an anime figure digging, with a karate chop, into the insides of a computer. This needlessly dramatic logo was drawn by the younger brother of my boss. The whole enterprise might have something to do with money laundering. We certainly don't have enough customers to keep the business afloat. And the boss flies back to Chiquinquira more often than seems strictly necessary to keep up with the family.

I don't know nor (given my financial state) care if this is 100% on the up and up.

Gustavo called again. Cole Porter. "Just One of Those Things."

★ ★ ★

I answered, talked, and hung up.

"He's at the school," I said, "but he's having a hard time retrieving the stuff from over there."

"Do you want coffee? Anything?" she said, looking at the black screen, the blinking cursor. The computer, its memory erased, reverted to primitivism, infancy, latency.

"Coffee's good," I said. She placed her hand on my shoulder on her way to the kitchen.

I had unearthed the contents of the hard drive by the time she came back.

"All there," I said. "Nothing's really lost. Not even the OS stuff."

"Oh," she said. She brushed her fingers near her eye again, crying without doing so.

"So it's." I stopped. I didn't know what to say. "It's all there."

"No," she said, handing me my coffee. "Sugar? I also have Splenda."

I shook my head. "Black's fine."

She stirred her coffee and inspected the spoon. She would not look at the computer or at me. Her knee pressed against mine.

I noticed her father's house for the first time: clean, tidy, spare, with a shelf of science books, the expected posters of Einstein and Hawking, family photos, nothing out of place, nothing out of order. It wasn't the house of a man who broke his daughter's heart—had he done so? I didn't know. I knew he was a widower. I didn't know much, I realized. What had transpired?

"Could you delete it?" she said. "I mean, could you delete it delete it?"

"No," I said. "I mean, I can. There's stuff I can do. But there's always a way to get it back." I didn't get it. She wanted it back and there it was, and now she wanted it gone. "You could take the hard drive out. Take a hammer to it. A drill. Even then there's ways."

She placed her hand on top of mine. "I don't want to know. I want to but I don't."

Neither one of us said anything for a long time. We drank her coffee. The computer whirred.

"Read it," she said.

"No," I said.

She squeezed my hand. "Please. A favor. From one Colombian to another."

I turned to Renee's dead father's computer. I suspected he had taken the breakup with grace. I had every indication that he had, but I feared looking in—I didn't want to run into child pornography or jpegs of atrocities or the scatological dreck collected by people who had lived, people who had existed and who had behaved as ordinary human beings. I approached every machine with the same tremor, the same dread, always afraid I'd see something I wished I had never seen, material I had a hard time believing a fellow human being would be interested in or turned on by.

What we found was a little stranger. I read for hours.

There was nothing objectionable in the drive or in the trash, and seemingly no anger in the several hundred e-mails retrieved from their temporary black hole. I was grateful for that, though disturbed by the sheer amount of material addressed to Renee's father's lover, who, as the correspondence made clear, was also Renee's dearest friend.

But there was, at least, it seemed, the absence of any real malice.

Here is a fable of the reconstruction.

Renee's father, a high school physics teacher, died seven days after the culmination of a stormy affair with Renee's dearest friend, another physics teacher at the same school. Renee's father was a widower, but Renee's dearest friend's spouse (a physical education teacher at the same school) was very much alive, and understandably pissed off. Renee's father died in his sleep of old age. Renee's dearest friend would no longer speak with Renee.

So she wanted to know most of all if her father was a ranter, an accuser, a paranoid. She knew that her best friend had ended the affair. She did not know why, and wanted to, or didn't, or sometimes did and sometimes didn't. She also wanted to retrieve these links, or to lose them—how they had hooked up, why they had parted ways. (The links are not necessarily always there. People communicated by e-mail to any great extent if they had stopped communicating sans clothes. Or not. They sometimes did and sometimes did not. Regardless, whatever the men decided to accuse the women of, in these e-mails, had often only a passing connection to reality.) Her father was not a violent man, and had by all accounts behaved, after she called things off, like a gentleman. He did not stalk. He did not call. He went to bed every night for six days and on the seventh he did not wake up.

The father spent all six days writing. He wrote nonstop.

I understood the impulse. I wanted to do the same thing. I wanted to write to the girl who broke things off with me five months ago.

Here's the thing: I had been alone for two and a half years, then briefly swooped upon by this girl—short, half-Portuguese, half-Scottish, with a sloped nose and green eyes. She swooped and, two and a half weeks later, dismissed me. I had been alone since then. I could not get the songs out of my phone, but that was all that remained of that radiant breach of my solitude. That and the ghost of hangdog gratefulness.

And anger. And humiliation. And the impossibility of anger—the knowledge that it seems inconceivable to be angry at someone I've seen naked, or who has seen me naked.

This rule is not universal. Half my job involves dealing with the data of people who do not go by this rule.

★ ★ ★

I read on. There were no indications of how the affair had started. None of how, exactly, it ended. But Renee had a good indication of the dates; the content of the e-mails changed drastically once the affair trailed off. The letters increased in length and became loose, disjointed, and hardly dealt with the world of the high school. They hardly seemed to deal with the actual at all.

Instead, Renee's father developed a gangly narrative about old men who wore pinstripe suits and controlled the world. They were like the Illuminati or the Masons. The e-mails explained that the organization, called Pragma, had developed ways to lengthen one's life without holding on to the bullshit of youth (Renee's father's word: bullshit), and that while this trick allowed them a kind of serenity otherwise unavailable, it also meant that many of the more senior members were senile. Hence the state of the world. The old men in charge had gone bonkers. They were chaste. They had no use for Viagra. (The father did. We found a few order confirmations from several online pharmacies.) They could levitate. They could make small objects float. They could make household pets talk for brief periods of time—days, sometimes weeks. They used to call themselves the Pragmatists and later shortened it.

They were all men and they were all old and they were working very hard to turn the reins over to women as soon as it became feasible. This turnover, the father explained, was crucial. The world would not last too long in the hands of men. Men had fucked it over. Had fucked it over until repair was next to impossible.

I tried to shape the information into a story, for Renee, the daughter. But it wove back and forth, and the e-mails lost focus, lost coherency.

But his main point was that women could fix it. They could buy pinstripe suits, have them fitted, tailored, and learn the requisite incantations, and levitate whatever needed to be levitated. (Several of the e-mails delved on the ceremonies at unnecessary length. There were animals involved. The animals sang songs, and the father included transcriptions, many written in minor keys.) The old men would yield their extraordinary power to women in their early twenties.

I could sense in the narrative a submerged intent. The father—while unraveling, while unthreading the fabric of his sane, tidy, orderly world—seemed to be trying to praise the woman he had been sleeping with. I think. I don't know. It seemed garbled and halfway coherent and desperate and possibly innocent and likely not and it made me queasy.

The world had been undone by the desire of men, he wrote. By what men did and said to spend time with women. The old men lost their chastity—or the chastity had never been there at all, it was all a front, or the intention was there but not the will. They were dirty old men. They pursued any pretty girl who passed their way. They used their powers— powers, the dead father specified, inextricably linked to the pinstripe suits—to make themselves attractive, irresistible, to these women. They grew distracted. They—

Renee's hand rested on my thigh. Her bare foot slipped on top of my sneaker.

Pavement's "Summer Babe." I switched it off. Pavement again: "We Dance." Gustavo both times.

They had decided to look for women of exceptional grace, intelligence and beauty. I cringed. I could see it coming. On the next message, I found it. Renee's best friend would, of course, be one of them. She'd wear the pinstripe suit. For a while I had tricked myself into thinking that what was going on was nothing more than a Henry Darger-esque narrative—a naive allegory, revealing more about the author than the author cared to reveal—an attempt to expurgate the remnants of the affair. He had not let go. Could not.

The old man wanted her back. Had he given any thought to his daughter (whose hand, as we moved to the next e-mail, had not moved from my thigh)? Had he thought of the husband?

Renee's best friend would be in the higher echelon of the Pragma community. The old men would greet her with open arms. The old men would not be there at all. The old men would be dead. But the friend would be there, in her splendidly tailored suit, part of the welcome committee.

I ran my left arm under her blouse and high up her back. Her right arm vanished into the unzipped V of my jumpsuit. I sat, she stood, and we faced not each other but the computer screen, our legs somewhat intertwined. This accidental pose reminded me of an illustration from the Kama Sutra—we were fully clothed, but what made me recall the handbook had more to do with how we resembled a pair set up for a specter opposite of us, some specter looking back from the bowels of the screen. We were reading.

She was crying. She did not brush the real tears from her real face.

The phone would not stop ringing. Modest Mouse. The one about the heart being a cliff and the brain the bitter buffalo. I answered. Gustavo talked. I listened, and hung up. "Gustavo got the stuff from the school computer," I said. "He found all sorts of other e-mails—most of them he didn't send. He just saved the drafts."

"More like this?" she said. We had untangled.

I thought of lying. "Worse. Threats, lots of—sorry. Just creep-type stuff. Lots of bad words, lots of threats."

She said nothing. I didn't know what to say.

"He didn't send most of it," I said.

"Oh," she said. She sat by the computer and said "Oh" again.

"I can delete this," I said.

"No. I want to read it. He was a good man."

"Okay," I said. "I should go." I did not have the heart to disagree, but she was wrong. Good is letting go. I had no clue as to how one let go—I myself had not done so—though I had not done what Renee's father had done. Suppose I wasn't good. Suppose goodness, in this department, was all a matter of degrees: that one slid up and down this scale, with the chaste old men in pinstripe suits on one end, and with the dirty old men, in equally natty pinstripe suits, on the other. But that one at least let people be if one did not let go. Cut off contact. Move on. Wish them well while all the same wishing them the worst but doing nothing—nothing at all. Let go. Let everyone go. Let's all go.

Renee walked me to the door. We shook hands. I never saw her again, although she called. I quit the job, but kept the jumpsuit.

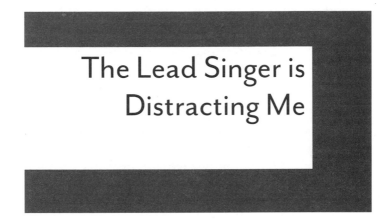

The Lead Singer is Distracting Me

The lead singer should really stick to the part where he sings and not come right up to me. I'm the guitar player, and I know that this is pretty much standard rock-and-roll practice, but it is distracting. It is hindering my ability to perform my guitar-playing duties.

Because it isn't like I was ever, like, into dancing—like having this really intense moment where the singer is half an inch from my nose and we're both doing the same thing, like we're Rockettes.

I am more about looking down at the ground and thinking about trying not to mess up. And hoping really hard that I am not about to mess up. It's hard! I play these arpeggios where I'm—*woosh*—all over the frets! All over! And then you have this jackass with bad breath right in your face.

The lead singer should brush his teeth, but that's neither here nor there.

Also, I am a guitar player. I am a guitar player because I like to stay in my room and play guitar. All the time. Pretty much from, like, age 10 till, like, five minutes ago.

If you are a guitar player, the whole point is that you are out there playing an instrument, which requires effort and concentration, which means you're not all that into people. And then you're touring, there's people everywhere, you're rushed onstage, and there's thousands of people all being way too loud—so it's stressful enough. And there's the lead singer, who never seems to have any of these problems, and he wants you to dance with him. And all you want to do is play the right notes.

Which is hard enough when you're playing as fast as we play. It is harder still when the lead singer does his air-guitar thing, like he's so into what you're playing that he has to play it, too.

But he is playing the wrong notes. He's just moving his hands around.

It doesn't matter that it's air guitar, since you are looking at him playing the wrong notes, and you're scrambling to erase those hands from your memory, and you're thinking, "I was only three credits short of the marine-biology degree. Dolphins are jerks, too, but they are not as inconsiderate as lead singers."

Also, personal space? Because it's not like we're all crunched together when we're playing *Halo 2* on the bus. Who wants to be all crunched together? Not the lead singer!

Which is why we are not allowed to look at him when we eat. When we're at McDonald's, he is to go in first, order, and then we can go in, but we are not to look at him. We are to sit on the opposite end and stare at the calorie counts printed on the paper mats. And so this is something, I think, that could translate to the stage.

We could all just stick to our respective spots. We could still rock, but we wouldn't have to move around so much and distract each other. The lead singer wouldn't get so sweaty, with all the jumping and air-guitaring and moving around and that desperate look in his eyes, that one that says *Please play along.*

It could be classy! Like when we had the symphony: The cellists weren't coming up to the violinists to show them how much they were digging what the violin people were doing. We should try it. Also, I would like more solos.

Errands

Rosalie's parents lived in a forest. Rosalie lived in an apartment complex. They lived in Oviedo, a city adjoining Orlando, many years from now.

Rosalie measured time by how many birds hit the window: Five in a row meant that it was late afternoon, and that she should be out. The phone rang—she did not pick it up, because the caller ID showed her parents' number. They were calling from the forest. If she could make it through her little one-day vacation without having to talk to them, it would be wonderful. She had very little money for food and did not want to share the little she had with them.

She needed to pick up some Shake 'N Bake—the forest where her parents lived lay between her apartment and the Publix supermarket.

★ ★ ★

The birds were small—and dun-colored, ugly, and dumb.

She put on the polo shirt with the Taco Bell logo from her job last summer and stepped out. She turned to her apartment and waved—she said good-bye to the TV (still on), her comfy chair (rescued a few months ago from a Dumpster, though she needed the help of a few people she didn't know too well from the factory), and her modest stack of Golden Books (she colored on the their margins with Crayolas, though the doodles did not stay fixed to the stiff, slick pages). She turned again. She waved to K., the naked woman who stood with the broom in the apartment opposite hers. K. waved back, though she was blind. How the blind woman interpreted Rosalie's mute gestures she never knew.

K. never closed her door. She was blind, but she was lovely. Rosalie was in love with her blind neighbor.

(She had told her as much last summer. She brought her tacos that she smuggled after she was done cleaning. The blind neighbor thanked her for the tacos, but refused to acknowledge her feelings. "You're a child," K. said. "You don't know what you want. You can't know what you want if you're eight or ten, or however old you are. How old are you anyway?" Rosalie held up all five fingers of her left hand, four of her right, and shook her head: she was in love; she knew what she wanted. K. said, "When you're as young as you are you don't know what you want.")

"If you're going out," K. said, "you mind picking me up some Advil?"

"Not at all," Rosalie said.

"You're a dear."

"I love you."

K. smiled and waved her off. She must have a terrible headache, Rosalie thought, and if she brought the Advil back and her headache was gone would the blind woman love her?

Would K. love her then? (It bothered her that she knew only a letter of her true love's name—when they first met she had asked her her name, and she had said K., and Rosalie had asked her if it was Kay as in Mary Kay, and she had said No, that K. was just the first letter of her name, and when Rosalie asked her what her full name was, K. had said, "I'm blind. If you're wondering why I'm walking around the house without a stitch on, that's why. Because why not?") You did not fall in love with your errand girl, did you? She walked down the stairs and knocked on her other neighbor's door.

"Jesus is my Jesus is Jesus," Umega Upsilana said.

The woman was older than K., and stouter, but beautiful all the same. She was tall and wore a pale-blue gingham dress, and she spoke to herself continuously.

"Hello! I'm going to pick up some Advil for K. Also some stuff? Other stuff? So I was wondering if, you know, if you needed anything."

Umega walked into the folds of her apartment. Rosalie waited outside.

If she married Umega the first thing she would do would be to clean up the place and get an air freshener and maybe throw out the cats or at least let them out once in a while, but if she let the cats out they would jump on the stunned birds and torture the poor things. She had seen them do it. They wouldn't kill the birds. They would paw at them for hours. If cats knew CPR, they would revive the birds when they were at death's door and paw at them again until they were at death's door again, and then they would readminister CPR.

Rosalie snapped the necks of the birds. They tasted odd, and she never plucked them right, but they were free-range— they were free. Besides, they were migratory birds migrating to nowhere; they were going from nowhere to nowhere, and they kept hitting windows and cars. They were suicidal and nutritious.

Umega returned with a shopping list scrawled on the back of a utilities envelope.

"Sure. I can get this. Also, I keep telling K. that I love her? And she keeps acting like I'm not serious. So if she's like that— if she's all oh-I-like-you-but-I-don't-like-you-like-you—then I want you to know that I would totally consider you? But we would have to do something about the cats."

"Jesus is Jesus. My Jesus."

"So I'll be back with the stuff." Rosalie pocketed the money Umega gave her. "And litter? Because you didn't put it on the list but you need it."

Rosalie tilted her chin and widened her pupils—she liked trying her Orphan Eyes on Umega because they had no real effect. Umega hardly looked at her at all. Umega hardly looked at the world, just the corners.

Rosalie had worked as an Orphan last Christmas. Grown-ups walked hand in hand with her from toy store to toy store in the mall and bought her things. She could keep the toys or return them and get a commission. They told her she could return for Easter if she wanted. She did not want to. It was an in-between job: after the Bell and before the razorblade factory. She was happier at the razorblade factory.

Because here was the thing: as an Orphan you had to pretend your parents had died, and they dressed you up in rags, and you had to be teary and snotty all the time, and there were days when no one would show up and you'd just sit there, waiting, doing nothing, talking with the other children, rehearsing your tales of woe and parental loss: random decapitations, plane accidents, lottery-ordained executions, cancer, AIDS, drug addictions, love triangles that resulted in terminal heartbreak, brake failures in ethanol buggies. It was too much work.

At the razorblade factory she packaged four razors into small paper envelopes. They gave her gloves, pink and imprinted with the logos of Sanrio characters: Hello Kitty, Pukka, Ponchi, Belial. Her co-workers, all about the same height and age, hardly spoke—they were so busy.

"I'm seeing my parents tomorrow," one of them (Martha? Maria?) said yesterday.

"Mine are dead," Rosalie said, not really looking at Martha or Maria.

They worked for an hour before the girl next to her, Irene or Izzy, said something. "You should hang out with me. I'm going to be watching TV all day."

"I don't watch TV," Rosalie said. The razors hardly ever caused an accident, and fatalities were rare. They had been well trained.

She packaged and thought of the women she wanted to marry, thinking maybe that they would hang out during her break, all the while smiling and humming along to the song piped through the speakers. She knew the name of it because they played it all the time and she had asked her shift manager, and he had found out for her from the people higher up: Schubert's Trout Quintet. She knew all the parts, and thought that maybe she could get it for her apartment—there was a kind of happiness in listening to the song and following it in your head, in lying to her co-workers, in watching the birds hit the window, in thinking about K. and Upsilana, and she could almost say what it was but not quite. She could feel it but not name it. It was a kind of daydreaming but not quite.

Umega closed the door and Rosalie found herself mentally adding the litter to the list of items. A bird had shaken itself back to consciousness on the patch of brown grass by her side. The bird fluttered into the air—it rose in a breathtaking arc interrupted, for a second time, by Rosalie's second-floor bedroom window.

Dumb birds. Dumb, dumb birds.

She reached the store at seven-thirty, the hem of her shirt rimmed with mud. She worked at the Taco Bell a week before they had begun providing uniforms her size, but her store had not lucked out, and she had been specially unlucky: all the manager had left were extra-large men's shirts. (She remembered talking to a union person who told her that it was wrong for underage children to work. Rosalie had told him that since '09 it didn't matter, because if you were over eight you were not underage anymore. Because of the resolution. And the union person had said that resolution or no resolution it didn't matter: she was underage. And she said no—not according to the law. And the union person huffed and puffed and moved on to the next employee, but the store manager spotted him and brought out the shotgun and the union person had to scram.) The polo shirts fitted her like dresses. She thought of them as dresses. Her Taco Bell dresses.

First she purchased K.'s Advil at the Publix drugstore so she wouldn't forget. She put K.'s change in her front pocket, then pulled the money Umega had given her from her shorts. She unfolded the utilities envelope and walked the wide aisles and plucked the various items from their nests—the candles to the saints, the Lotto ticket, the Clamato, the thin envelopes of freeze-dried steaks, the cans of tuna fish, the cat food, the litter, and the Shake 'N Bake for the birds. She also bought herself a small square of government chocolate wrapped in the white and green colors of the supermarket.

The bags were heavy but not heavy heavy. Not like the bags of frozen beef at the Bell. Not like the sour cream and the guacamole.

On her way out she patted Hairy Seldom the dog. She liked the dog. Whenever she had some time she would sit down next to him and chatter away. She pretended that the dog talked back. Like she would say, "Oh, but it's such a hot hot day and I've got such a long way to go and I'm sure I look a mess." And the dog would be like, "Oh, no, you look lovely. You are such a lovely girl and you look really lovely in that dress—specially lovely—and any girl who married you would be so-oh lucky." And she would be like, "Oh, you!" And Hairy would say, "Really, like you're Saint Di or Saint Bleeth: that lovely." And Rosalie would giggle. Saint Rosalie. The dog didn't talk, of course. Dogs don't talk. It just sat there with its stupid happy Lab face and smiled at Rosalie. Publix had stenciled the dog's white fur with the supermarket's sans-serif "P" logo in mint-green on its back and stomach. The dog sat there and smiled. But you could sit right next to him and pretend. He smelled like the strawberry shampoo she smelled on the dirt they had rubbed on her rags, when she worked as an Orphan.

"I'm so tired," she pretended to say to Hairy. "So-oh tired. But it's cool because today and tomorrow I don't have anything to do. Nothing at all! I can sit at home and watch TV. I can play Parcheesi with K.!"

"I'm happy for you," Hairy said. "It's good to sit around and do nothing at all. It's my favorite thing! It's what I love doing all day! And, by the way, don't you look particularly lovely today in your lovely, lovely dress."

"Oh, you."

She patted the dog and left the supermarket via the sliding doors that had stopped sliding six months ago when they cut off the A/C. Dark already. Her favorite show would be on soon. She would be late for it unless she cut through the forest. She did not want to go through it. She did not want to run into her parents.

★ ★ ★

The forest was not dark or scary: It was well-lit and easy to navigate. The trees were tall but mostly leafless and had been planted in neat symmetrical grids. She would be home in no time at all if she followed the path and avoided the golf balls that had exhausted their arc and tapped and pocked at the trunks and at passersby, and besides, the light from the branches hanging high overhead was more reliable than the flickering yellow splotches of the street lights—so she dove into the path. She thought that maybe this time she could pretend that she couldn't hear them, but she knew she could not. She walked down past the shed, hoping that maybe they wouldn't be there, but they were there, of course they were. They heard her, and she them—she heard them call her out ("Our daughter! Our darling daughter! Our Rosalie!")—and she thought, Maybe I'll just pass by and they won't go after me, and maybe they won't cry, but she heard their slow weak steps behind her, their sad shuffle on the dry dun needles, and she heard them sobbing, so she had no choice but to stop, though she didn't turn around— they wouldn't make her turn around—she heard them sobbing, asking why she didn't stop by more often, why their darling Rosalie didn't even call or mail them a postcard, some sign that she was alive and doing well, and by the way how was the Taco Bell job working out, and she told them that it wasn't, that she had quit but she was doing okay at the razorblade factory, and that she was making a good living, and she would soon be married to a lovely woman with a physical impediment.

They said, "Oh, we are so proud, so proud of you, and do you have, do you by any chance have any . . . Do you have any. . . ?"

Rosalie tossed them her little square of chocolate and some of Umega's change, which she hoped Umega wouldn't miss, and she said that she had to get going if she was going to make her show, and they said, Okay, fine, but write or call. Stop by.

"I will," Rosalie said. She waved good-bye and ran out of the woods and into her apartment complex.

★ ★ ★

After the first commercial break she was seized by panic: she had forgotten the errands. She had left the bags in the forest. And if she were to run back they wouldn't be there any more. The bags would be gone.

But no: There they were, on the kitchen counter. She picked up the Advil and Umega's bag and walked through the patio and into K.'s apartment, who was watching the same show. K. thanked the child with a distracted wave. Rosalie ran downstairs and knocked at Umega's door. She handed Umega her groceries. She gave Umega what remained of her change, and Umega said, "Jesus! Jesus is Jesus," which might have meant Thanks. Or it might have meant, Where's the rest of my change?

Rosalie responded to K.'s wave and Umega's words with the same silent burst from the day before: the happiness for which she had not found a name, but which she had felt on saying good-bye to her parents. She recognized something else in it. She still did not have a word for it, but she thought it was a lonely sort of happiness, or a happy sort of loneliness.

When Rosalie returned to her apartment the show had just started again. A heavy indistinct object (a safe? a piano?) fell on a person. It was very funny. She sat, happy to find that the show had just began as she had returned—it was such a perfect summer thing, such a wonderful little gift from the universe to herself during this short vacation, this gift of good timing. The phone rang. She picked it up and hung it up without looking. And she was so happy—it was so good to be back home.

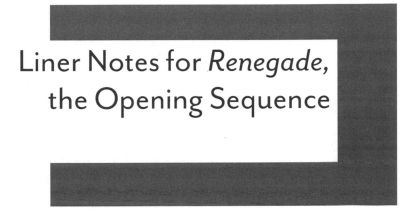

Liner Notes for *Renegade,* the Opening Sequence

The original version of *Renegade*'s opening sequence is fifteen minutes longer than the length of a single episode of the show. While this sequence could, in fact, be reconstructed, little would be gained by doing so; the opening-sequence director was aware that an hour-plus of Lorenzo Lamas riding through the desert was too much, but he was also, he later admitted, mesmerized by a long shot of the motorcycle (looking no bigger than a pebble) progressing from one end of the screen to the other—punctuated by dust storms, sunsets, and surprisingly inspired (and inspiring) music.

The director never showed this version to the producers, but he screened it for a friend, a substitute teacher in Culver City, and later the two had a falling out (the sub called at all hours to see if the director wanted to hang out, eat pizza, watch some Seijun Suzuki, and it was all very sad and needy and eventually got old, so the director screened his calls and there was an ugly confrontation, about which the less said the better), and eleven years later the sub called him out of the blue and said, "Dude, *Brown Bunny*," and hung up.

Which indeed the original *Renegade* sequence looked a lot like. Granted, *Renegade*'s music was synth-ish and uptempo, and there were awkward shots of Lorenzo looking straight at the camera dissolving into stiff slow-motion shots of a leg kicking a villain, glass breaking in that stiff pause-and-progress Post effect to stand for slow motion but which just feels wrong—anyway, none of these elements make their way into *Brown Bunny*.

But none of the better elements of the original opening sequence do, either. The cut submitted to the producers was five minutes. The cut seen on television clocked in at three. While both share the same voiceover ("He was a cop. A *good* cop. Until he was set up by cops. *Bad* cops . . ."), the shortened version cornered the Renegade into a one-note righter-of-wrongs and solidified the whole riding-through-the-desert-on-a-motorcycle-and-righting-wrongs thing, though viewers will remember that Lorenzo did little riding through the desert in the actual show.

The original, on the other hand, sought to broaden the Renegade's range, though the same problems surfaced: many of the elements present in the opening sequence never really made it into the story arcs of the show.

One could argue that the Renegade also never read to blind children, and so showing him doing so, in the opening sequence, was unnecessary. But why not?

There is also a brief shot of the Renegade taking one of these blind children for a ride on his motorcycle, all the while still reading to the blind child, which connotes in equal measures cojones and devotion. Also cut was the Renegade learning motorcycle repair at his local library. On his table, about to be checked out, we can see *Motorcycle Repair for Dummies*, *Zen and the Art of Motorcycle Maintenance*, *E-Z Harley Repair*, and of course some other books, a thick biography and a novel about coming of age or self-discovery or rural life interrupted by violence and sundry tragedy—the point being twofold: to explain how the Renegade managed to travel around and do okay before meeting his support team (the fat man, the man of certain ethnicity, and the hot blonde); and also (and most importantly) to broaden and deepen the protagonist's emotional/intellectual range. Because, sure, he might be out to right the wrongs of the world, but he also cares about literature. Because that is the type of guy he is. And also the part where he is at a recital playing the Goldberg Variations. Because—again—that is the type of guy he is.

Or was. Since the sequence is no more. Or is, perhaps, after all—after all, viewers know that the Renegade reveals depths unexplored elsewhere: humor and love and valor and compassion.

Nobody is lobbying for the reintroduction of the sequence to the soon-to-be issued DVDs—it might do as a bonus feature, but that is it. Besides, you can view it at the Los Angeles Museum of Radio and Television, and it can also be located in the production company's vaults. It only takes a few letters— more than one, yes, but no more than four—requesting a videotape, and lo, it will be delivered to your doorstep. You could also, I suppose, Google it. It's out there. Everything is.

Hobbledehoydom

The nineteenth-century novelist Anthony Trollope almost certainly did not sleep with his friend Kate Field. She liked him. They corresponded frequently. They saw each other as often as they could, which, given that Trollope lived in Britain and Field in America, was not often. Trollope was enough of a public figure to generate some tabloid press over the non-affair. He was happily married, and faithful. For all that, I have no doubt there were times when Anthony and Kate sat across from each other and he wished she would jump out of her chair and into his arms. Kate was stunning, funny, an early feminist, and altogether formidable. He wrote of feeling his heart flutter in her presence. Everything remained platonic—the novelist had often written about hobbledehoys, and at the core of hobbledehoydom there is a commitment to reasonableness, a tempering of one's acts if not one's thoughts, all born out of terror in the presence of beautiful women. So he sat. Had he moved at all, Kate might have responded favorably.

Who knows? He did not dare. He was a putz, a coward, a Charlie Brown, a hobbledehoy.

I discovered Trollope's novels during the worst of my hobbledehoydom, while living in Bogotá and dropping out of various universities from 1993 to 1996. Not even Trollope, by the way, could find a way to place a hobbledehoy in the center of the action—in his novels they often play second fiddle: quiet, incidental, well-intentioned, but inept.

Finding a mirror in Trollope's world pleased me to no end, but it did not happen right away, nor did it keep me from fucking up royally, over and over again, as I pinballed between schools, skipped classes, and fooled myself into thinking I was cooler than I was—that some measure of hipness was being achieved, and that something was accomplished by my drifting, by writing for an English-language weekly that paid poorly and late and whose checks often bounced, by teaching a few English classes for just enough money to keep me at a ratty boarding house in Chapinero Bajo, hoping to overcome my Charlie-Brownness via beer and books and obscure music and unbelievably cool acquaintances. The awkwardness remained. I could not approach women. I tried to imagine a past filled with innumerable conquests—when in a bar, I tried to set my face like that of a man who has seen it all, done it all. I drank and learned that, in Colombia, women in bars would pull you onto the dance floor and did not care if you danced, did not care if you wanted to dance, did not care for you particularly. By some kind of institutional democracy, everyone at a given table, at some point or another, would have to dance. Their job was to make sure this happened. They held you close. You told them you didn't know how to dance, so they led and you followed. I never slept with any of them. At that point I had never slept with anyone—I'd fooled around some, and was already aware that at 20 I was woefully behind the curve, and ungainly, and timid, and, worse, I'd been away from

Colombia for four years so I spoke with a half-gringo accent that sounded affected and irritated even me.

When it finally happened a year into my return, in 1994, it happened as I hope it happens to everyone, hobbledehoys or not, with a mix of wonder and alarm and surprise, an unutterable burst of bliss. But even then there was a feeling of an unearned reward. I remember waking up, or not waking up so much as stirring from whatever approximate sleep one achieves when lying next to a body that has only recently become familiar, and being hit by the realization that people did this all the time, that regardless of any evidence to the contrary, this was a perfectly ordinary thing. When it ended, it ended more or less well. She was 36 and had uneven teeth, was recently divorced and in great shape—a Colombian woman who spent most of her time in company of foreigners, so our brief time together, two Colombians in a cluster of Anglos, hinged on a kind of fascination with this group we had stumbled upon. I was 21 and had grown a beard.

Trollope maintained that one grows out of one's hobbledehoydom while never having grown out of it himself. The truth is one adjusts. One learns to live with the limitations and advantages of hobbledehoydom. The Colombian woman and I ran into each other at a party a few months after we broke it off and I was thrilled to see her, and she seemed happy enough to see me. She looked more beautiful than I remembered—out of reach once again—and had a boyfriend she had picked up at one of the language institutes where I taught: tall and fair, way taller than me. I drank too much. I puked off a balcony and accidentally knocked some plants over. Hungover and sour, awkward and sad—once a hobbledehoy, always a hobbledehoy.

Immediately following this paragraph is another one that also begins with waking up next to a woman—British, 27, engaged. But first a few problems need to be addressed, the first being that this essay should be less about monkeying around and more about the hobbledehoydom, where the latter leads to a paucity of the former. The second is that in focusing on these moments I distort those three years. I jump from one bed to the next in the space of a paragraph, whereas if done to scale, several blank pages would separate one encounter from the next with, granted, a few smallish exclamation marks added here and there, minor instances of drunken contact at expatriate parties. And yet these are the only moments that seem to matter. Another problem is the whole sentimental education angle. There shouldn't be one. Despite the one minor epiphany dotting the end of the next paragraph, what I learned from that encounter, from any of these encounters, really, is little, or little other than that they're probably one of the best things about being alive. No sentimental education angle exists. No education. Just waking up, once in a while, not really understanding how it happened, next to an implausibly beautiful woman in the north of Bogotá.

In 1994, I wake up next to an implausibly beautiful woman, Mina, in the north of Bogotá. She's British. Twenty-seven. She's into 10,000 Maniacs, is trying to read García Márquez in Spanish, teaches science and math at a private school, is witty and sweet and easygoing. I'm still 21. Her apartment is clean, spare, has two floors and an invisible roommate. I don't see the roommate once in the months I'll spend with her.

The night before, the first night, before I knew that it would be the first in a series of nights, we'd been at a bar with a group of British and Irish people I didn't know too well— they all had real or real-sounding jobs: stringers for the *Christian Science Monitor* and *Time,* translators for Café de Colombia and smaller enterprises, a few freelance writers who also doubled as instructors at English-language schools, a few legitimate teachers locked into contracts for private schools. The expected amount of drinking occured. Everyone danced. Late in the evening, she took my hand and led me to the floor, and soon leapt—leapt, literally, bounded—into me, knocking me flat onto a table and knocking down a couple of empty Aguila bottles and aguardiente shots. She pulled me up from the table and kissed me. We were drunk, making out, doing nothing that is not done by everyone at one point or another under the influence (and of course, yes, without the influence as well, but the influence helps)—and the only claim I can make for including it here, amidst all the hobbledehoydom, is that it is rare for one of us hobbledehoys to happen upon this situation.

We don't leap, not even when drunk. We are seldom leapt upon, but are graceful, I think, in receiving the leapee, or if not graceful (knocking down things, being knocked down ourselves) we are grateful. A great deal of sloppy dancing followed. As we left, a good friend of hers grabbed my arm and reminded me that not a week ago I had puked in her living room (true), and that I should be good to her, the British girl who has leapt into my arms, the joke being that I owe them on account of the puking, but her grasp makes it clear that she is not really joking. I nod. I feel sophisticated, worldly. I know exactly where this is heading. It heads exactly there, with one brief pause, in the taxi, where she has to roll down the window to vomit.

We're up. She walks to the bathroom, naked and lithe, and while she's in there I read a poem taped to the wall, printed in block letters next to a photograph of her and a guy. Other photographs have been pasted to the wall. Friends. Coworkers. Snippets of England behind them. The poem is not much— trite, sentimental, plodding, something about her face in the moonlight, written by someone who is clearly nuts about her. She returns—bobbed black hair, green eyes, smelling of the

Body Shop. We kiss. She has brushed her teeth. She tells me about her life back home. Family. School. Pets.

She talks about her fiancé, the boy who wrote the poem, the boy in the photographs, and explains, before I ask (and I wanted to ask, would perhaps have asked, maybe not), that they agreed, given her 10-month contract, to see other people. We kiss again and she offers me breakfast (I decline, I don't know why) and we exchange numbers and I leave, bowled over by the practicality of this couple, their pragmatism, a kind of hard-nosed nonromanticism that is, in its own fucked-up way, sweet and almost romantic. Just as I am about to leave, I realize I know nothing of how the heart operates. I know nothing of my own heart or of the hearts of others—even the most ordinary couples (in one photograph they looked like the least exotic pairing in the world) inhabit a world I do not understand, don't have a key for.

I ran out of cigarettes the night before. As I leave I ask if I can bum one, and she says she doesn't keep them in the house, she only smokes when she's drinking, it's a filthy habit she's trying to quit altogether. She also says she wants to see me again. We kiss once more.

We see each other for the next three months. It trails off, and while it does, while several blank pages await, I should get back to Trollope. Actually, this makes sense because it is while the Mina thing is losing momentum that I first hit upon Trollope in the British Council library.

Know this: We won't get back to the British Council library. We jump several novels ahead of the first one I read by Trollope. And know, too, that I will keep edging away from what should be the meat of the essay—though you will find a long quote by Trollope on what makes a hobbledehoy a hobbledehoy, nothing will follow on my own immobility, my awkward pauses and silences, my inability to engage. Nothing on the months spent alone between each encounter. Nothing on the frustrations inherent in knowing that the bulk of these encounters are, for the women involved, transitory—the hobbledehoy as a way station or rest stop. Nothing on how little the situation has changed, post-1996. Not even so much as an acknowledgement of the whining going on here: which, come on, if you lack the courage to initiate any kind of contact and still find yourself messing around, even if it happens rarely, even so, somewhere in here there should be a nod to those who try and try and try and, because of bad luck or the ambivalence and randomness and unfairness inherent in the rules of attraction, fail, or those who don't try and are not swooped upon, ever. Nothing on failure. Nothing but a bitter little coda on shyness and immobility.

Several hobbledehoys appear in Trollope's novels, but none as Charlie Brownish as John Eames, who shuffles into *The Small House at Allington* almost apologetically and falls in love with Lily Dale, a girl as lovely as one would expect, given the name. John gets engaged, by accident, to someone he shouldn't, falls heavily into debt, drinks too much, but later whips up into shape, discards his disreputable acquaintances, becomes an honorable civil servant, all right before heading for Lily Dale's place to have his heart broken into many small jagged bits. Trollope allowed himself the satisfaction of having Lily marry no one at all, and in *The Last Chronicle of Barset*, the novel that followed, he would keep Lily and John apart despite hundreds of letters from readers pleading for marriage. (The other suitor in *Allington* is a genuine asshole. John, while a schlep and often prone to asshole-ish behavior, remains for the most part clueless but sweet. In *Barset* John comes close to losing h'doydom—but traces remain.) Trollope knew the heart of his hobbledehoys, and he knew the hearts of the girls hobbledehoys fall for. In *Allington* he provides as good a summation as one could hope for on John Eames, and on himself, and on me, and on every other hobbledehoy who has ever walked the earth:

I have said that John Eames had been petted by none but his mother, but I would not have it supposed, on this account, that John Eames had no friends. There is a class of young men who never get petted, though they may not be the less esteemed, or perhaps loved. They do not come forth to the world as Apollos, nor shine at all, keeping what light they may have for inward purposes. Such young men are often awkward, ungainly, and not yet formed in their gait; they straggle with their limbs, and are shy; words do not come to them with ease, when words are required, among any but their accustomed associates. Social meetings are periods of penance to them, and any appearance in public will unnerve them. They go much about alone, and blush when women speak to them. In truth, they are not as yet men, whatever the number may be of their years; and, as they are no longer boys, the world has found for them the ungraceful name of hobbledehoy.

Such observations, however, as I have been enabled to make in this matter have led me to believe that the hobbledehoy is by no means the least valuable species of the human race. When I compare the hobbledehoy of one or two and twenty to some finished Apollo of the same age, I regard the former as unripe fruit, and the latter as fruit that is ripe. Then comes the question as to the two fruits. Which is the better fruit, that which ripens early—which is, perhaps, favoured with some little forcing apparatus, or which, at least, is backed by the warmth of a southern wall; or that fruit of slower growth, as to which nature works without assistance, on which the sun operates in its own time—or perhaps never operates if some ungenial shade has been allowed to interpose itself? The world, no doubt, is in favour of the forcing apparatus or of the southern wall. The fruit comes certainly, and at an assured period. It is spotless, speckless, and of a certain quality by no means despicable. The owner has it when he wants it, and it serves its turn. But, nevertheless, according to my thinking, the fullest flavour of the sun is given to that other fruit—is given in the sun's own good time, if so be that no ungenial shade has interposed itself. I like the smack of the natural growth, and like it, perhaps, the better because that which has been obtained has been obtained without favour.

But the hobbledehoy, though he blushes when women address him, and is uneasy even when he is near them, though he is not master of his limbs in a ball-room, and is hardly master of his tongue at any time, is the most eloquent of beings, and especially eloquent among beautiful women. He enjoys all the triumphs of a Don Juan, without any of Don Juan's heartlessness, and is able to conquer in all encounters, through the force of his wit and the sweetness of his voice. But this eloquence is heard only by his own inner ears, and these triumphs are the triumphs of his imagination.

That middle paragraph, the one arguing for the superiority of hobbledehoys, is mostly wishful thinking. But we do improve with age. We can't get any worse. We grow more aware of our limitations, our flaws, our fatal passivity— we stop trying to pretend we're someone else, and if it isn't growth it's a gentle resignation, the dawning that we were probably old and feeble and weak on the inside anyway, so all we're doing is growing into the face and the body of our inner Charlie Browns. We weather the indignities of old age better than those who had something to lose in their youth. We were undignified to begin with. We know how to deal with it. We improve on the sloth and ungainliness of our early years. (I'm 28 and in better shape than then: I could beat my 21-year-old self, no sweat, smash him to a pulp with my fists, or I could outrun him. I do about 120 pushups every day. My former self could do none, didn't know that exercise mattered, was bored by that kind of physical activity, thought he knew everything there was to know—it took him a while to wise up. Not that I'm anywhere near wising up enough. We're slow learners. Mostly we learn that we don't know much. We learn that we need to learn more. But Trollope is wrong. I detest the smack of natural growth. I'm terrified of 30, and of how time keeps rolling and of how nothing remains fixed.)

Our looks improve. We were always plain, and time adds nothing but character to that plainness:

Kate Field was much, much younger.

Anyway, I kept on reading and writing, and somewhere

in the middle of all this inactivity— all these blank pages, all those days wanting women but unable to do much about it, being swooped up only on rare instances— I happened upon one of my favorite Sundays in Bogotá.

The newspaper I worked for, the *Colombian Post,* subscribed to the Reuters wire service (no Internet for us in 1995, not much of one). I assembled my pages with odd bits from the service (themed snippets: animals found in inappropriate places, inept Brazilian thieves, that sort of thing), with hastily written fluff, and with film and book reviews that only a few oddballs cared for (a nervous flyer discovering the paper in an Ecuadorian airline—she wrote a few letters from different airports, an ex-embassy worker living in Cartagena). But my coworkers and I always suspected that the *Post* was a front, a laundering operation, because our circulation was pathetic and no one believed even those low numbers. We didn't think we had any readers.

That Monday I'd written a real article. It started as a cursory tour of bars in the Zona Rosa neighborhood and turned, by chance, into a straightforward account of 10-year-old flower girls, underage street vendors, and the men who controlled them. Mostly it was straight reportage. The kids, their stories. The acknowledgment that some of the stories were clearly made up on the spot, fabrications to induce sympathy but masking stories as sad and terrible just beneath. I'd also done the layout and the photograph.

On Sunday, the day our newspaper was distributed, I walked to Oma, a wildly overpriced boosktore and cafe, to celebrate. I bought a copy of the the *Miami Herald*—the cheapest English-language daily they carried—and a cup of coffee, and sat down with my pack of Marlboros. I was hung over, red-eyed, unshaven, a seedy penguin. Two American women sat down at the adjacent table—lovely (thin, fit, hair cut short) and well-dressed, one a blonde. They had purchased copies

of the *International Herald Tribune* and the *Colombian Post.*
They flipped through the *Post* until they happened upon my
article and read it. I watched them read it. They seemed to
like it. Of course I didn't say anything, wouldn't have dared
say anything, but it didn't keep me from feeling elated. This
isn't much of a moment to end on. It isn't much of a victory
or a vindication. It isn't much of anything. But watching them
read felt wonderful and impossible and meaningful. It felt like
contact.

We end more or less where we began. The man at one
table, the two women at the next. Charlie Brown on the bench,
the little red-haired girl on the other side of the cafeteria. Or
Anthony in the parlor, sitting not too far away from Kate. No
one moves. No one says anything. Nothing happens.

My Sister's Knees

The Palonegro airport lies on a flattened hill dwarfed by the scrabbles and vertebrae of the cordillera—a death-trap, a speck of gray in a riddle of roads and greenery: the Bucaramanga airport. My home town.
I don't travel well.

I don't travel well, nobody does. Some are better at it than others, but if you ask your friends, the people you've known long enough, they'll tell you about their hell ride, the bad flight, the turbulence, lost luggage, fights, dyspeptic flight attendants, or unexplainable heebie-jeebies, the last being the worst because no clear reason can be given, just the texture of terror without the text. Everyone, even seemingly fearless travelers, has a bad-flight story.

Here's mine: landing in Bucaramanga, my hometown, the plane shot up after the initial descent, and the pilot told us over the intercom that he had not seen the runway. Not seeing the runway was a big deal, but what did it was the pilot informing the passengers, informing me, of this foible . . . Fear of flying, I've read, is mostly fear of not being in control. So? Two planes crashed in Colombia that year, one belonging to an American airline, one crash a month after the other.

That wasn't why I didn't go back this summer.

I've been terrified of planes for four years. That hasn't stopped me. It wouldn't. I keep coming back. Colombian airlines are very liberal with their in-flight drinks.

My homesickness, however, is now tempered by relief at not having to fly, but of course that relief is soured by guilt about feeling the least bit happy about not going home, which inextricably makes me wish I were back home, and then I remember I don't have to fly, so I'm relieved. We could go on.

It has been a season of funerals and breakdowns, this summer, a heavy wave of unhappiness washing over the people I know in Orlando, maybe over the city in general. Brushfires have sprung up. Animals in a new theme park are dying, a reverse Noah's ark. Convenience store holdups now require more hostages than ever. It hasn't rained. Televangelists crawl out of their radio stations and UHF crannies, into campuses and street-corners, and their gospel is shriller, more bitter, more urgent. One of these fellows hired a hit man to do away with another, his lover's husband. Summer makes for impatient people in lines. Complaint departments are overwrought.

My friend Carol has been complaining about very minor things for the past two years, the whole time I've known her. She was diagnosed as bipolar a year ago. What I assumed to be charming quirks of an essentially solid personality have turned out to be signs of mild madness.

Part of the problem with life is that its most dramatic moments occur offstage. We are not privy to the best and the worst in others, and if we are it is only as witnesses or unreflecting participants, off to the side, extras in a production for which we've only been provided a fragment of the screenplay. With Carol's breakdown, I only have the before and after, not the during.

The after's cruelest effect has been on Carol's bottom, grown to absurd proportions from the cocktail of psychotropic drugs. The blonde waif who modeled for hair shows is now grossly out of proportion. When I first met her, I didn't find her all that attractive: a thin shrill girl with bobbed dry hair, wearing baggy jeans and a puffed black parka, to be transformed, during one of our first outings, into a rare and photogenic beauty, still perhaps more alluring in the abstract than in the flesh, of which there didn't seem to be much then. Now there's more than enough.

As for the before, I have some explaining to do.

She drank too much. Drank until she scrambled to the bathroom and puked and passed out. Drank and scrambled to the bathroom and, having passed out, made me kneel: beside her by the toilet, holding the airy strands of her hair and feeling through that insubstantial stuff the fine and fragile contours of her skull. Drank and scrambled and forced me to carry her to the bedroom where, drunk myself, I once fumbled a parody of foreplay, which she gracefully (teeth brushed, puked-on clothes changed to red satin underwear) brushed off, done so beautifully and with so little awkwardness that I realized that this girl, three years my junior, had been brushing off, must have been brushing off the same sort of fumbles for most of her pubescence, and waking up the next day I was rewarded with a hungover angel resting lightly on my shoulder. She woke up. I rubbed the tingling from my shoulder. She liked champagne.

One night her friend Christine drove down from West Palm Beach. Carol and Christine looked so much alike that Carol used a copy of Christine's driver's license to buy alcohol—she had reported it lost and received a duplicate. Well into the night, a Dr. Demento CD endlessly playing "Champagne," Carol tongue-kissed Christine ("Would you like to see us kiss?" she asked, though she did not wait for an answer), and she had Christine strip to her undies to show me the tattoo on the small of her back, a grinning mushroom, after which they headed to the bathroom to powder Christine's ass, the dark and the drink and the makeup smoothing stretch marks from her three-year-old pregnancy. When I told her that she looked gorgeous, baby or not, she said that she didn't understand how women could grow into fat cows just because they gave birth, that all that was an excuse for laziness, that she did aerobics, and still did, and had burned most of the fat in the first two months—she was twenty-two. She slid one kiwi-sized breast from her bra and pinched her nipple, undid the bra and rubbed both, inches from where I sat, and ran off to the bathroom afterwards and came back with her clothes on. And Carol ran to the bathroom and threw up, and then threw up some more. In the morning we drove to the International House of Pancakes. I bummed a cigarette from Christine; we crossed arms and lit each other's.

The next time I saw her, months later, she had a mermaid tattooed on her flank, and her hair was longer, teased and frazzled and ashen.

Christine's little girl I met in between the mother's two visits. They lived with Christine's mom, and one night they found the grandmother in the tub bleeding from the wrists.

Christine sent her daughter to Carol, and Carol brought the kid to class, a doll-sized munchkin with her mother's large brown eyes and fair and messy hair. We walked the length of the campus, Carol and I holding the kid aloft, making a tiny V out of her arms—we bought her ice-cream, listened to her chatter, an insanely beautiful child born out of a beautiful mother, an insane grandmother. I thought that this kid could might as well be mine and Carol's, that if we ever got together this would be the sort of child we would have, fair but not overly so, a little rugged, blond and darkish. It was an artificial family but it worked for that day. It felt good to be walking around with a pretty girl and a munchkin.

The kid left. Christine came and went. Carol had her breakdown.

During the tag end of the semester, she began to miss class more than usual. And after a while we stopped returning messages, stopped talking on the phone. Months later, talking to a friend of a friend of Carol's, I heard about the breakdown. I called her. She said that yeah, she'd gone nuts. I asked her what she had done. She said that she had tried to kill herself. She said that yeah, she guessed she was pretty nuts. I asked her if there was anything I could do. She asked me if I could drive her to the Fashion Square Mall. I said sure.

Her living room smelled of cat shit. Clothes and magazines were scattered about. The air had the stale and unhealthy density of a sealed chamber. The room's centerpiece, a grotesque pink sofa filched from her high school's theatre production of *Alice in Wonderland,* was streaked with strange organic stains, and Carol dangled from it and waved and apologized for the mess, which she said wasn't due to the fact that she was nuts, even though she was, but because she'd been lazy these past few days. Which I understood. Neither she nor I had taken a shower in days, but her hair was far greasier than mine. She walked to the bathroom and showed me how she dried hers using baby powder, lightly tapping, brushing, fluffing, tapping again—would I like some? I would not.

We drove to the mall. Along the way we caught up. She complimented me on my car and on my driving, both of which I was apprehensive about. I drove an '88 Hyundai Excel, bought by my parents the last time they visited. They were here for a month and figured it'd be cheaper to buy one than to rent one, and that I'd have some sort of use for it afterwards, notable because, like most economy cars, it crumples into a ball in wrecks, and compacts its passengers, turns them into dead bits and pieces of their former selves.

Cars and planes scare me, though they fascinated me as a kid. When I manage to fall asleep while traveling, I dream the same dreams I dreamed in planes and buses when I was eight, dreams where I walk deserted streets and enter hollow skyscrapers. The word bears endless repeats: dreams, dreams, dreams.

Driving along, we caught up. She hinted at a relationship she was having with a Dominican drummer I know, and she said that ever since she was on the drugs she was getting fat, and the previous drug they had her on cut off her need for cigarettes, but that the need was back; she lit a Camel Light (my brand) and rolled down her window. I told her I'd quit. She puffed and puffed as we rode to the mall.

That summer I did fly back, and the flight was predictably hellish.

Our house in Bucaramanga stood a block away from our country club, where my sister swam and my father played tennis. My father dreamed of a revolution. People in ragged clothes broke windows, fired guns, stormed houses—and in the dream he saw himself and the family and our friends holed up in the club, an enclave of sanity. I told him how the dream reminded me of the movie where a small crew finds shelter in a mall and fends off zombies, George Romero's *Dawn of the Dead*. He said he remembered himself telling me about the movie when he first saw it, when I was four and we lived in Caracas. I think I remember that, too. Not too many years ago, a friend and I rented *Dawn*, which had the washed-out, lurid colors of any film from the seventies. It was also terribly and terrifically graphic and, more so, tapped directly to a common nightmare, the sort of phenomenon you were deeply familiar with, without recalling where, exactly, you had been exposed to it, the alligators-in-the-sewer meme, the same vague terror shared by frequent flyers.

My sister has flown all over Colombia, has covered most of the North-American southwest. She has even been to Cuba. She is a serious heavy-duty athlete, a swimmer. When we first hugged, she cried and told me how much she missed me, and a couple of hours later she was crying for real. She is sixteen.

She had a knee operation five months ago and is still recovering. Her times are sluggish, well below the marks she was making before her knee popped out on a tennis court—she is now terrified of stairs and of running on hard surfaces. She is also irritable, quick to snap, a bad mix of hormones and frayed nerves. The dedication required of any serious athlete borders on the neurotic, the obsessive, and wears thin and badly on teenagers. She's doing okay. Better. She's doing better. We took a cab to the hospital to meet her doctor. He examined her knee and told her that they might have to do another operation by Christmas. She cried some more. She said that if she had another operation she would never be able to get her times back. There is something wrong with her ligaments—too flexible, too prone to give way; she would gross us out by stretching her pinkie, arching it till it met her arm. She told me that, right before she went under the last time, the light in the operating room took on a life of its own.

I had gone back to smoking shortly after last seeing Carol. I thought I'd quit again before visiting the family, but I could not.

I had to step outside of the house to smoke, but it wasn't something I kept at all secret—I was through with secrets, or with most. My father walked out and met me by the sidewalk the second day. He watched me smoke. We talked. It is impossible for me to enjoy cigarettes when I'm with the family. When I'm away it seems necessary, but when I'm home it strikes me as a stupid habit, not just the motions per se but how awful it tastes, really, after you and your lungs have had enough and it's just the reflex and the craving. So we talked. He asked me how things were going at school, and I said okay, better, better at any rate than before. Before is something we don't talk about.

What happened was that I'd dropped out of school in the US and returned to Colombia, and in Colombia I did about two semesters and gave up, and taught at shabby English institutos in Bogotá, and after three years I was fed up with that, so, without telling my parents, without telling anyone, I took off to the States on a tourist visa and disappeared, vanished for five months. Of course I called them when I was finally broke. Of course they helped out.

This is what we don't talk about—what we really and truly cannot talk about. I try not to think about what parents must have thought.

The prodigal son.

We talked. I told him about Carol while we sat by the curb, the concrete lamp-lit, all surfaces mottled, the leaves fluorescent, a procession of ants pallbearing a moth along a crack of the sidewalk. I also told him what I'm now saying about this particular summer—how a sad heavy wave had broken over Orlando. He asked me how I was feeling. I told him, not bad. I said that I felt pretty good and was half surprised when I realized that I meant it.

When I think of Colombia I see broken bottles glued to bright walls. Hardly ever do I think of what the country is actually supposed to be about, and when I do it's not unlike my father's dream: shreds of an overexposed film.

Home is where the heart is. The eye is somewhere else.

It has not rained in ages, and what that means is heatstroke and private invocations. Rain dances. What that means is.

The shortcut from home to campus is a lot behind a strip mall. The shortcut from home to fast food and a used-CD store is scaling a chain-link fence. The shortcuts from home to the houses of friends involve things I have not done since I was eight.

The shortcut from home to here is a short flight.

Fear of flying is fear of letting go. It is an acute case of backseat driving. My sister doesn't trust the ground anymore. I don't see why she should. I don't see why any one of us does.

Carol showed up yesterday in overalls and a white top. She's closer to her real size. I asked her if her apartment was still a mess, and said that yeah, it was, but that she was cleaning a sector of it each day, a couple of square inches, and that she had fought with her parents, and that she didn't want to go back to school, and she asked me how I was doing. I said okay, better.

It was four o'clock in the afternoon, the sky a patchwork of gray, makeshift clouds promising a rain that failed to fall. She told me that she hated this heat. I said that I did not mind it much.

I was thinking of what happens when you see your knee give way—what goes on in your head when you realize that your body might have some design flaws.

I had asked my sister if the operation had hurt. She had said no, not at all. She said that it was as though it was happening to someone else. When I asked Carol about the suicide attempt, she had told me the same thing.

The Spooky Japanese Girl
is There for You

You lose your credit card

and call the company, but no one answers—and that hissing noise? The Japanese girl ghost. You say "Hello?" three times. Then she hangs up. You shiver . . . What's that? A replacement card. In your *wallet.*

You're on a date

and trying too hard. You drop a knife, and there she is, underneath a table—pale arms, red dress, long black hair covering her face. You jump back. Your date says that you look like you've seen a ghost. You try to laugh, but can't. Your date thinks you're a complicated man, a man haunted by a dark, interesting past. And you are. You are haunted by your past—also by the ghost of a Japanese schoolgirl.

★ ★ ★

You're at the gym

and slacking. You think you'll do 15 minutes on the treadmill, then call it a day. But you look up and the spooky Japanese ghost is on CNN complaining about broken borders and how no one cares about the middle class. You run for a full half-hour, fueled by righteous indignation.

You're at home

and it's late, you're tired, and none of the light bulbs you've just replaced are working right: they flicker, they cast shadows that look like people or birds or household appliances. You're in bed, the TV tuned to static because you were so angry about the war on the middle class that you canceled your cable, and you're looking at the ceiling. The Japanese ghost crawls from one corner to the next. Her hair still covers her face. She moves in bizarre, halting steps, crawling to every lamp in your house and adjusting every bulb until the bedroom is bathed in a soothing glow. You sleep and forget to turn off the lights. The spooky Japanese ghost does it for you, then vanishes, never to appear again. Years later, you're walking down the street and spot a small distant figure in a red dress, and you run to her and—never mind, it's someone else. She's gone, you miss her, but ghosts move on: They can't hang around all day. They've got things to do.

Big Wheel, Boiling Hot

Karen said that we didn't have the budget for the five additional dancers, the live cello player, the four-piece string ensemble, the percussionist, or the costume upgrade. I asked her if she'd mind my looking around for additional investors.

She said that she didn't understand. Why bother? We had the score on MIDI. We had enough to cover everything with half the house booked. We just needed a couple of retiree busses and a lucky burst of ticket buyers: grandmothers taking their children out on a special night, misguided first dates, inexplicable anniversaries, and the people who will attend any event as long as there's singing and dancing and an all-you-can-eat intermission buffet. The show would open in two days, she said, and as stage director it really wasn't my business, though if the show was a flop of course it'd be my business.

I didn't say this. I grunted and looked for money from somewhere else.

★ ★ ★

I had never worked for a dinner show. There are plenty in Orlando, but after I dropped out of film school and put everything into the big failure, after working a string of crap jobs before settling into assistant manager at the Oviedo Blockbuster, these live theater shows with actual living people saying things they didn't mean had become invisible. I love movies. I don't understand why people would want to bother with a form of entertainment with no cuts and no frames.

So I didn't notice the billboards on International Drive for Arabian Nights or Dolly Parton's Dixie Stampede. I also didn't see the backlit signs on strip malls, the ones for wedding plays where the audience eats and pretends to be sitting in a chapel and not next to a Radio Shack, or where someone's been murdered and everyone's expected to take part in finding out the responsible party, the actors speaking in British accents for no convincing reason.

Karen is a slight woman, very pale, in her mid-forties, and often when I am asking her a question she is looking elsewhere, plus the lights are dim, so it took a while for me to realize that her eyes were very green. She must have been very beautiful. She does not own a cell phone. She is often on the theater phone, the one that takes reservations, talking to Mark, her boyfriend, a sixty-year-old bearded man who invested in Lou Pearlman's boy-band company many years ago and came into some money, some of which is funding this production.

The boyfriend is hardly ever here. He bought the theater for her. That is, he owns the theater, but he only really owns it—would only put out the money—because of Karen. The last time Mark was here was because one of the front door's large glass panes had jiggled loose. He duct-taped it back together and asked us not to rattle the door too much.

Karen's boyfriend's name is needlessly confusing because the theater was once known as the Other Mark—because the previous owner's name had also been Mark and because there were two competing dinner theaters of the same name in the seventies; the other dinner theater was also owned by a Mark, a different Mark, who first named it after himself, then changed it to Mark I, then Original Mark, then joined the Moonies and for a while simply took out all the signs and nobody knew what was going on inside.

Later, after he left the church, he put back the theater's first sign, the one that said Mark Theater, but by that time no one was interested and the place closed down.

Our place is now known as the Orlando Dinner Theater. It's as old as me, both of us being born in 1972, though I was in South America then.

Lord knows I've been here long enough, though, a fat muddling shadow since 1996—a college drop out in two continents, a minor footnote in *Mystery Science Theater 3000* (the failure was broadcast with running derisive commentary in the show's own last shadowy season, the one that aired in sputters over two networks, the one that wasn't particularly funny). We have both, the theater and I, managed to do not much of anything in thirty years. This coincidence in age often sends me to the archives, to look at the 1972 pamphlets and programs. They are as poorly put together as the ones we have now. The paper is brittle, as is Karen, and all I can think on this year—the year I'm about to hit a third round decade—is that neither forty nor sixty should strike me as terribly old, because it isn't, and that I shouldn't be thinking that these people should have done something with their lives already, because I have not. All the same, here is a great mystery: Why are people—no matter the age, no matter the technology—so bad at designing, diagramming, and presenting their printed material? The stuff back then was ugly, as ugly as what we have right now—a jumble of fonts, a jungle of poorly reproduced photographs and clip-art. Take, for example, the clip Karen chose for our current cover,

which takes some stretching to figure out is a worried secretary, though it might as well be Karen herself, since her hand is often pressed against her forehead, and she's constantly frowning, one small thin blur of concentrated worry, and she keeps telling me we have nothing to worry about, that I shouldn't worry so much, that I should relax, all signs pointing to trouble.

The back pages of these forlorn programs are little catalogues of failure. All these headshots, these capsule biographies, and all these people look bright and gleaming and undefeated, but there's nobody here you'd know. Some apparently made it to soap operas. Some appeared in movies I recognize—*Zardoz, The Deathless Devil, Willow, Apollo 13*—but whatever roles they played must have been small. One line, maybe two. They were here. They loved this or that. They traveled, sang in cruises, lived in Ireland or New York or Cincinnati. And then Orlando, and they were here for a month, in 1983, in 1979, in 1991, and the trail grows faint, and all I know of them is this small black-and-white testament, their face no bigger than my thumb. I keep an eye out for Karen and find her often enough. In her various headshots I find confirmation of her beauty. It was there. And it's gone.

The problem is that, until the new money comes in, I have way too much time to spend in the archives. There is a part of me that wants to go in, storm into rehearsals, and make the show really really good—I am sure I could do it. Instead, while they go over their lines and their blocking, I go to the archive and look at their predecessors. I am thinking, Why hope? All the while I am hoping.

I am also thinking of Robertson Davies wearing his cape in Oxford. He was twenty and sure of himself—just one fat Canadian in the middle of England, one lonely bearded guy convinced of his genius. I am not fully convinced of anything, but I do weigh three-fifty, and I have grown a beard. He wrote, he acted, he moved around, he flew from continent to continent. My family moved from Colombia to Orlando, then they moved back and I stayed.

Forty is not old. Sixty is not old. Karen twirls the impossibly long telephone cord and it follows her from box office to stage to backstage, Karen nodding to her boyfriend/business partner, drinking from her giant water bottle, and all the lights dim, the rooms dusty, tired reds, defeated yellows. We are doing *How to Succeed in Business Without Really Trying*.

They have rehearsed for three days (I was hired five days ago), and right now Karen is calling the *Orlando Sentinel* and a couple of other newspapers to tell them that the press screening has been cancelled. The actors know their lines, but Karen, the director (who is also playing the ingénue), has been changing the blocking. The stage is small, rickety, and all the props are school desks painted Day-Glo.

We all come in from other jobs, the actors mostly waiters and waitresses or BFA students from my old university, and they all go to great lengths to take the production seriously. They talk about their characters, invent a past for them, go through their lines again and again. I remember Penelope Fitzgerald's *At Freddie's*—the lone boy jumping to his death again and again and again, doing his King John bit. And then here they all are, four twentysomethings and gaunt forty-plus

Reefer Hare, a pockmarked spring of a man in the lead, and Karen, and the way they talk about the play you'd think it was life or death. They move in the tiny square of the ancient stage. We open for real tomorrow. They say their lines, the light filtered by dust unswept since the seventies.

None of us has received a paycheck yet.

Karen keeps her oversized bottle constantly filled with water and stalks down the hall, the cord trailing and desperately keeping up with the mouthpiece. I follow the cord to give her the good news, which I had just told the college students, all blondes, all of whom were effusive and kind and one of whom hugged me, though I was sweaty and heavy. She said she liked my cape and asked if she could wear it and I said no. We will be opening in eight hours. The four-piece string ensemble waits at the cafeteria at the corner of the strip mall, and I keep huffing and yelling Karen's name, but Karen does not turn around. She is wants to know, from the mouthpiece, if it is for real.

"Are you shitting me? Are you shitting me? You are shitting me."

I follow Karen into the empty green room.

"This cannot be for fucking real. You are shitting me."

It is only when Karen turns around that she realizes that there's someone else in the room. That is also when I realize that Karen's water bottle has some vodka in it. The smell comes from the open lip, from her mouth and from the mouthpiece, and from the sweat drying off on her arms, her neck, her brow. She ignores me. I follow her as she stalks a circle round the clutter of the green room which, like the rest of the theater, is not green at all but a golden mist, thick with amber dust, every surface draped with translucent scarves and plastic beaded shawls, all soft and cheap and beautiful. Karen keeps saying that this cannot be for real. I do not understand why we're sweating—the theater is kept cold. I want to tell her about the money, but now does not seem to be the time.

The problem of course is that now we have less than a day and though we have enough for everything I wanted, I have a hard time getting her attention. I might as well not have talked to my manager at the Blockbuster, who talked to his manager, who all eventually agreed that a community event of this sort would be good for our branch.

"Karen," I say.

She stops. Before, I had merely waved my arms around, tried to move in her field of vision, had even made a grunting sound. What I had to do was say something. Her mouth is open. Her breath is not unappealing, but too sweet and cut with the brace of vodka. I stopped drinking four years ago, right around the same time of the big failure, right around the same time most would have started, thinking too that I'd begin working out, that I'd get my life together and my finances straight and my ducks all in a row—go back to school, get a haircut, a girl—and here I was, with a woman deeply creased, deeply worried, deeply drunk. The room is all gold and red and mirrors. We are surrounded by short fat bearded men in capes, who are all telling a thin wraith of a woman, who is still holding the mouthpiece, that we have enough for live music, that all that's needed is the sheet music. Do we have it? If not, where could we get it?

"These guys are good," I say. "I heard them. They could go through the whole thing in an hour, at the most."

Our MIDI score has scratches. It's been recycled from a previous performance in the mid-eighties. Even our leading man showed signs of emotion when I told him that I'd found us live accompaniment.

Karen has not closed her mouth. Her hair has been recently cropped. She had been in *Peter Pan* fifteen years ago, playing the eternal boy—the photograph showed her boyish, and there had been more copies of that particular program than any other, but I don't know if it was because she cherished that show or because it had flopped and nobody had come and so we were stuck with more of those than any other. She had been a beauty. The phone clicks, stands still, then goes through its little hang-up birdsong.

She asks if I have the money on me, and how much. I grunt. She takes the grunt for a yes, which I suppose it is.

The thing is, she tells me, is that we have to pay the rent on the theater. We had to pay it about two months ago. I tell her that I thought that Mark owns the theater.

"He does. We're not," she says.

The green room is very warm. I should be elsewhere, anywhere else, even standing behind the Blockbuster cash register and dealing with people's crap choices in movies.

"We're not speaking," she says. She looks at the phone.

It's clear—from how she was speaking, what she was saying—that it couldn't have been anyone but Mark. It is also clear that you should never trust a liberal arts major with money. Doesn't matter if it's theatre, film, anything. You might as well abandon it in a reservoir, under a bridge, and if you come back in a week and some of it is there—whatever wasn't pecked at by ducks or washed down to some ocean far more beautiful and pure than whatever you wanted to create in the first place—hell, if even half a bill is there, you should be grateful.

"I told them I'd be paying them today," I say, thinking I should have lied and told her that I had already paid them. That the money is out of my pockets. Which it isn't. It's right there. All she has to do is reach.

"They're closing us down. I can't fucking believe they're doing this to us. I keep thinking they're just fucking with us but they're fucking not. Fuck me. Fuck this. I cannot believe they are fucking doing this to us. Fucking Mark. And they won't give us any more money."

This is where I sort of begin to understand what's going on. It becomes easier the more she unravels, because you can put more of it together with the sputter of drunken confetti. Mark apparently had not much in the way of money, but was desperately in love with Karen. He'd been taking out loans on his stake of the Pearlman company and making payments on a mortgage Karen had taken out on the theater, in Mark's name (and without Mark actually knowing), for a previous production which she thought was going to be a moneymaker—it wasn't—and so when Mark found, later, that Karen had been using the *How to Succeed* money for something else, neither the mortgage nor the rent, that is when their troubles began. All this happened months and months ago. And the calls were partly whatever couples talk about but also Mark desperately trying to figure out what was going on, financially. She had been telling Mark that she had been paying the cast and crew with the money. She had been telling the cast and crew that the money was used to cover production costs. And nobody knew how fucking hard it is to fucking manage a fucking theater at a time when nobody gave a rat's ass about a fucking theater, or the fucking arts, or her.

"Karen, where's the money?" I feel like we've been in the room for hours and hours. We've been here nine minutes. "The checks? Reefer's been borrowing rent money from his girlfriend for all September."

Why Reefer? Why do I know this? I talk to him once in a while but, given that he's the lead and thin and has a girlfriend and people seem to like him, I couldn't really care less. Fuck him. But there I am, talking to Karen, thinking of Reefer Hare in the cheap gray suit, looking at himself in a fake mirror, just a poorly hammered wood frame framing nothing, you see through it into the wings, singing about how he believes in himself—how he's this young guy going straight to the top. And he's not. He's not young. He's not going anywhere. The voice is strong, though, and through the rehearsals and lunch breaks and every moment he had, he kept rehearsing, adjusting his imaginary tie in front of the imaginary mirror, saying, "I believe in you." And the chorus of old men, whose lines are all about how they were going to stop him, had to stop him—but really, do you need to? Really? Because it seems to me we do just fine stopping ourselves. The old men. All I could remember were a couple of short lines, either fifties slang or musical-theaterese for someone bright and eager and ambitious: big wheel, big beaver, boiling hot.

She sobs and wipes her nose on my cape. "It's hard. Are you kidding me? It's so fucking hard."

She takes another long unhappy gulp from her water bottle, and I remember coming in early to work and finding her just ending her morning run, her legs strong and resplendent with sweat, the outline of her sports bra dark against her shirt, and taking big greedy gulps from the same water bottle. So I was thinking, No way. No way she's drinking so early in the morning. And it doesn't matter how much of a drunk you are, there's no way you're drinking your way through the rent and expenses of a small theater company. There's no vodka that expensive.

She has not stopped crying. "They're going to close us down."

That's when the front door is broken down—the sound carries even into the recess of the green room. Broken glass. People shouting. Threats to call the cops. Someone asking where the phone is. Karen and I hear it all and she asks me once again for the money. Later, it turns out that at least one of the BFAs and Reefer himself knew how badly off we were. Karen was not good at keeping secrets. And she'd been promising money all around. Every week, she kept saying it'd happen next week. All the same, and much as I love the idea of a big incident, some giant to-do, it's still hard to take in that people would actually break down a door, or that they'd even be able to. It was nothing anyone meant to do. Reefer locked the door and one of the men knocked so hard and, less because of his strength and more to do with the building waiting to fall apart, dislodged the pane, all the duct tape coming loose, and it fell on the theater lobby—one giant crash. And the screaming grows louder, Reefer of all people insisting that they have no right to be here, the men saying that they do, that they're foreclosing on the damn thing. The finances are murky, but murkier still is the procedure, which seems off, which makes me think whoever Karen did business with was not the best choice. There were probably better bankers out there.

Soon it won't be just her and me in the green room.

Karen's about to repeat the part about how she can't believe it, how this cannot be happening. My musicians are eating kugel in the corner cafeteria, and they are bright and still in college and working for close to nothing. I tell Karen that we should play on—just tell the ticket-holders to meet us somewhere, anywhere, and it'll be a coup, a fucking hoot, it'll work. It should at the very least get us some publicity. We go, we do it. The show must go on. I actually say, "The show must go on." I don't even think about it, then I do, and then I realize that I have yet to actually hear the show from beginning to end, and that it's not so much the show, or the people involved. I don't know what it is. I grunt.

Maybe it's this: If you put it in motion, you see it through.

I tell Karen we have to see it through. We have no choice.

Karen nods. Then she asks for the money.

The last I see of her is two nights later, on the local news, after we find out she had been collecting payments even after the bankers closed down the place. It's in the consumer fraud protection segment, the ones with the camera chasing a shady element, some swindler, down to a car, and there are always hands blocking cameras, or hands hiding faces, and there's always that awkward chase, one person wanting answers and the other simply wanting to get away.

With Karen it was no exception. She was chased, she covered her face, she jerked the camera away. She was asked what she had to say to all the disappointed ticket holders. They had interviewed some of these ticket holders, old couples in shiny jackets, minutes before, and they really did seem, surprise, disappointed—then and only then did I consider the possibility that we might have provided actual entertainment, as in actual entertainment to an actual audience. She said that they'd have to talk to the bank. The interviewer said that they had—that apparently Karen had been collecting the money. She said that they could not be for fucking real, with not enough of one word bleeped. That she had no idea where the money went. That all she was trying to do was bring art to Orlando.

I believed her. That day's shift at Blockbuster had been brutal—hours of standing and doing nothing. The dinner theater people had dispersed. They had all gone to their other lives, and the musicians were paid at least, and I thought of Reefer, our gaunt leading man, walking with me to the cafeteria after we were shut down, talking about a part he had landed at the Rep for next month, and about his girlfriend, and about how much he liked his new character. We were leaving the ignominy of Karen's bankrupt world for the buzz of traffic, the exhaust of bars and franchise restaurants, walking down the sidewalk into more modulated and far brighter noise. It was all good and lovely and stable. It was here to stay. That was what I imagined Karen was driving toward, in that last shot from the news, her small red Honda driving fast and hopeful into the ordinary.

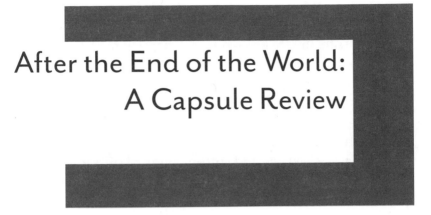

After the End of the World: A Capsule Review

Enterprise Carolina sits at the edge of the end of the world, and she doesn't know it. These are the first few months of the Event: Clocks and timers have slowed down, the Swedish rock band Roxette has made a comeback, and talking cats are making sporadic appearances—also some Seraphim.

Enterprise Carolina carouses with mountain bikers and Hell's Angels. She wears shitkickers. After dinner she gathers her gang of fellow fifteen-year-olds and contemplates vandalism in the half-empty malls of Culver City.

They beat up old men! They shoplift from The Limited! They return shoplifted items to the store and (brazenly! brazenly!) demand a smaller size, a larger size, a different color! They stare down older girls and giggle at their weight behind their backs! They fill up on samples from the food court! They loiter by the fountain!

They wear leather and dog-collars, fishnet stockings cosmetically torn, heavy mascara, and silver and silverette chains with skulls, monkeys, Celtic crosses, and the suggestive tongue logo of The Rolling Stones. Their hair is dramatically gelled. They sulk. They do not like you.

Their performance is not without problems.

Enterprise Carolina is a bit too beautiful. One feels uncomfortable with this hyper-eroticized depiction of a teenager, balanced as it might be by Carolina's dramatic revelation to Lozenge Carmichael—sidekick—that she is a virgin and will remain so until married. Carolina is pure and has a heart of gold—is this what we need for the days after the end of the world? Should we not be stepping away from this queasy mixture of hard-edged grit and cotton-candy idealism?

And what of the design choices? Enough with the Mad Max clones already. So the world ended. Fine. But why do we—all of us—feel the need to wear clothing that is dusty and torn, and patched together willy-nilly?

The Wal-Marts and the Gaps are still running. Why not go there? Have we lost our zest for tasteful outfits in our collective wait for judgment from some Supreme Being? Must we own wolves? And why drive souped-up cars welded from makes both domestic and imported? And why decorate them with spikes, gun turrets, and shark fins?

Time has become unmoored, and we are no longer at the whim of mortality. Fine. The old men who have been beat up will get up in the morning and have their coffee, unbruised and sprightly. I'll still be writing this review. Enterprise Carolina will still haunt the streets of Culver City—she will march under the yellow and red backlit signs of Indian, Thai, and Cuban restaurants, and she will walk to Sony Studios and make obscene gestures at the movie ads, at the tourists, at the cats who just can't seem to shut up. I don't think we should be overdramatic, is all.

It is not overdramatic, however, to rhapsodize about Enterprise Carolina's beauty—to say that she will be a stunning woman when and if time begins to move forward again. That she might abandon her life as the leader of a wild outlaw gang. That she might pursue college and get a degree in liberal arts. That her golden hair and crooked smile and street smarts have won the respect of Capsule Reviewers everywhere. That she is dazzling and worthy of admiration, stomping in her shitkickers into the haze of this fiery perpetual sunset, fading from us as we take our notes and make appreciative comments to fellow Reviewers. That she has enthralled us. That she is remarkable in a time that is anything but.

Five stars. Five golden stars. Five golden stars and my heart.

Debtor

We were sitting around, my family and me, all of us not being disappointed at how I turned out, when my uncle brought up Ricardo Niebla. My wife and I had been in the thin air of Bogota almost a week. We were almost used to the lack of oxygen. It was my wife's first time in the country.

"His brother lives across from us," my uncle said. "He hasn't paid his rent in half a year."

I used to work for Ricardo and vaguely remembered his brother, Santander. He had done something in government but made most of his money as a middleman in hostage negotiations. Both brothers shared the same aquiline nose, the same love for double-breasted navy blazers. If I were to run into Santander right now, I'd mistake him for Ricardo. Or maybe it would be Ricardo, visiting his brother, and I'd tell myself, No, that's not him, and I'd walk right past him. It's likely he wouldn't recognize me either.

I'm not the only one who has changed.

My aunt and uncle lived in the same apartment in the north, with the same stunning view of the Septima, but my five cousins were gone, all of them off to Canada or France. My parents had fled as well. They lived in Texas, my sister in Florida. We had all arrived at the same decision at different times. We moved, we aged, and Colombia stayed behind. Susanita remained extraordinarily elegant. It helped that she was tall, regal in her Japanese silk robe and despite the oversized, sneaker-shaped fuzzy slippers she wore around the house. Camilo Jose stood two heads shorter than her, his Amish-style beard turned white with age. He was in remission from prostate cancer, his left eye turned milky and no longer working. He staggered when he walked and was frequently out of breath. "He's never complained," Susanita told me on the day they drove us to the Salt Cathedral and to Andres Carne de Res. She said it when he was out of earshot, not long after they bickered about stopping the car at a colonial plaza so my wife could photograph it from the back window. "Never once," Susanita said. She helped when he needed help. Otherwise they were the same as when I left them thirteen years ago.

I expected to see everyone. I expected the lot of my past to return to Colombia along with me after so many years away, but we are never so lucky, never so unlucky. My wife and I had honeymooned in Kauai two years earlier. We flew to Thailand and Cambodia the year before. She kept saying, "We should go, we should see your country," and I agreed. We should see my country. All the while not wanting to. Wanting to and not wanting to.

Part of the problem was staying with Camilo Jose and Susanita. They had been too kind to me when I was living in Bogota. It was my first time out of sleepy Bucaramanga, my hometown, and it was my first time away from my folks, and I kept dropping in and out of school while writing for Ricardo's English-language newspaper. My country proved too much for me. I told everyone that my novel was getting published, that I was going to New York. None of that was true. My novel wasn't very good, and I'd only written thirty pages. And instead of New York, I flew to a friend's couch in Orlando, Florida, from where I did not move for three months. I didn't call my uncle and aunt. I didn't even call my parents. No one knew where I was or what had happened to me. No one even knew how I'd been able to afford a plane ticket.

Well, Ricardo knew. My check from the newspaper had bounced, so he offered me the plane ticket in exchange. I had taken the ticket. We were running ads for Avianca's new Bogota–Miami route.

At the bank, a Conavi, the teller who witnessed my distress when the check bounced, said to me that everyone there was familiar with Ricardo's account, that checks bounced left and right but money came in and out. So, she told me, we could keep trying to make the deposit. You never knew, it didn't hurt to try. Was I crying? I might have been crying. I'm no longer sure, it was so long ago. It was all the money I had, this money I didn't have. And I already knew: I was done with Colombia, done with the newspaper, done with pretending I was going to classes and getting a degree in writing, because why would you need a degree for that anyway? You wrote, you read, that was all.

The check finally cleared, but by then I was already on the plane, so I was paid double, not exactly through ministrations of my own. Blame the sweet sympathetic teller, not me. There was real pleasure in the act, nonetheless, particularly since that hadn't been the first bounced check Ricardo had given me. Some of us waited months for payment. I figured I was due, was owed. Plus there was a small measure of satisfaction in leaving the country a criminal.

I flew. I smoked on the plane—one of the last times you'd be able to do it. I played bingo with the passengers and the

Avianca flight attendants and won nothing.
   I did not come back.

The Conavi no longer exists. The bank's bee mascot, black and
yellow and cheerful, presided over the digital clock and ther-
mometer that marked the northernmost end of the Avenida
Chile. I forget what took its place, who bought it, but I still
remember the jingle, the smiling bee.

It's not entirely true, my not coming back. I visited the very
next year, and Camilo Jose hosted me and an American friend,
and my uncle hardly looked at me the whole time. What he
said to me, on the night we were to leave for Bucaramanga,
was, "You lied." He also said, "The newspaper wants its money
back. They keep calling. I tell them you don't live here, that
you never lived here."
   Which is true: I had given them my uncle's number because
I didn't have a phone at my boarding house in Bogota. I told
my uncle I'd take care of it, and I never did.
   And then I never came back, this time really. Truly.

My aunt is, in fact, disappointed that I no longer call myself
a writer, but she is not too disappointed. I am not too disappointed either. What I do these days is the opposite of writing:
I tidy up WordPress templates. I work for the communica-
tions division of Pittsburgh's largest health provider network.
I remove the *Lorem ipsums,* the filler text that isn't quite text,
and I resize the columns to fit our content. I check the style
sheets for inconsistencies or potential problems. People ask
me if I'm a designer, and I say no. People ask me if I work with
computers and I say yes, I do, but who doesn't these days?

I spend the bulk of my time erasing and clearing. It doesn't feel like a job, like something you'd get paid for, but I find it soothing.

My wife has asked that I keep her out of certain parts of this story, for reasons which may become clear in a moment, so the conversation I had on my way to see La Javeriana, the university I dropped out of three times, is maybe one I had with myself and not with my better half.

I could no longer imagine my old self in Bogota. Couldn't really imagine being friends with him. Had my wife been there, walking the Septima's monoxide-clotted sidewalks, she would have wondered the same thing. Back then, would we have been friends? Would we have even liked each other? That's the kind of question to which you reply "Maybe." What you really mean is "No." But that was a whole other life, a whole different person.

Bogota had also changed beyond recognition. I couldn't even find the building where I used to work. We put the newspaper together every week and went to drink Aguila and eat empanadas in the tiendita next to the office. I remembered that the building huddled a few blocks south of the Chile, not far from the Septima, but we walked a ways and nothing felt familiar. Later, my uncle, who knows his real estate, explained: Developers tore down anything under five stories and replaced it with taller, newer, more profitable buildings. Our decrepit, tiny office never had a chance. I imagined the building moving in the night, walking away, a little hobo pack trailing it, in one of the thousands of nights I was in another country doing my best to forget this one.

At the Javeriana, we couldn't get into the better parts of the campus. They've locked down my favorite green space there, and guards ask for your ID and will only let you in if you have a good reason to be there, which I did not. They check for weapons and explosives in every bag and every purse. Not just there but when you go into a mall, when you walk into a store. Susanita dismissed these searches. She said they don't make anyone safer. That if anything they make everyone feel less safe, as though something terrible were about to happen again, though nothing has. Nothing too terrible.

After trying to see my almost alma mater, we zipped to the top of Monserrate—the first time I could afford taking the cable car. I last shuffled up the mountain a heavy smoker who'd drunk too much the night before. Grandmothers with debts to the Virgin passed me on their knees. I was in better shape now—my wife and I are both joggers. But we still weren't used to the altitude. We made it to the top of the mountain and looked out at Bogota spread below, its vast network of red brick and its ribbons of green: the trees, the parks, the gardens. I made out the Plaza de los Toros, where I saw my first and last bullfight. My wife asked me what that was like and stopped me almost immediately, saying she was sorry she'd asked. A protest was getting underway below. We could hear it, though we were five hundred feet above the city. It felt like we were way higher. A large crowd rumbled unseen, unhappy, indistinct enough that we'd never know what they were unhappy about.

It was when we went back down on the cable car and returned to the Candelaria that I ran into Ricardo's brother. This is the part that my wife has asked to be kept out of.

Let's say she stayed at the cafe that belongs to the French-woman. There are two cafes, one owned by the francesa, one by her former husband. Let's say my wife and I had an argument, which happens, which totally happens to traveling couples. Let's say she stays behind and pets the cafe cat, whom we

saw through the Plexiglas covering the open interior courtyard. The cat did his little cat-dance on the roof and padded
down to the patio for us to feed him, to pet him. Let's say I left
my American wife alone in the cafe in the middle of the Candelaria. I said something dismissive about my country. She
was offended on my country's behalf. It could have happened.
People do fight when they travel. Maybe we fought.

The streets of the Candelaria are colonial and narrow and
choked with tourists, and many are still paved with cobble-
stones, but Colombia's administrative heart lurks nearby, so
you find government functionaries too. You also find hangers-
on. Pickpockets, artists. Nuns. Priests. Flocks of schoolkids in
uniform. The whole thing, in spite of the new condos and the
tasteful boutique hotels, still resembles a set: Colorful Colombian Street Life as Allegory, with Every Aspect Represented,
from High to Low. What I'm saying is that there was a mass of
people, no one staying still, and it'd be highly unlikely to spot
a familiar face in the movement and the bustle as wavelike and
perpetual as the flight patterns of the Plaza Bolivar pigeons.
That I'd recognize someone from thirteen years ago felt almost
impossible. Even more so when you consider that the person I
recognized was not someone I knew well—Ricardo had been
my boss, not Santander. Santander I'd seen on TV and only
once or twice around the office.

And now here he was on the Candelaria.

Santander had no official connection to the newspaper.
The brothers had gotten together to fund a treasure-hunting
expedition off the coast of San Andres island, where a couple
of Spanish galleons supposedly ran afoul of the British in the
1600s. The Spaniards tried to evade the British and ran into a
reef or a shoal and sunk, and their doubloons sank with them.
Supposedly. The brothers hired a dodgy Russian crew. They
commissioned what Ricardo told me was a submarine but
what I imagined was something much smaller and humbler.

The Russian crew hung around the newspaper bullpen for weeks. "If anyone asks," Ricardo said, "they're reporters."

Our Russian bureau.

What was shocking was seeing how little had changed. Santander wore the same double-breasted navy blazer. His dark hair was slicked back. He did not look much older. I had no cause to talk to him, particularly because I had every cause to avoid his brother. A part of me believed that Ricardo was still looking for me, still calling my uncle, thirteen years later, insisting on the return of the plane money. All the same, I found myself following Santander.

We passed the capitol and the Justice Palace and had our bags checked by the Military Police. No cars could go in here, the mayor safe in his palace across the street.

I followed Santander into the Santa Clara museum, the dimly lit former Colonial church, thinking still of the Russians in our bullpen, of sunken treasure. I waited for my eyes to figure out that we were no longer in the haze of the city. We stood until the paintings revealed themselves, every wall adorned with oils, the altar decked in gold, the room heavy with the smell of durable pigments and wet stone and wood. The church had stood since the sixteenth century, its art piled on top of itself until Colombia realized that there was too much in here, one priceless panel of Colonial art crowded into the next, and that no real church service could be conducted— not if you wanted any of these archangels to survive—so they turned the church into a museum. No flash photography allowed. A pieta hung next to another pieta, angels hovering above both. In one, the donors who had commissioned the painting had made it into the painting themselves. They awkwardly framed the virgin and her dying son: a husband and wife with hands folded in prayer, wearing frilly cuffs and looking out of place, like they'd Photoshopped themselves into the scene, staring at you, saying, Sorry for photobombing Jesus.

They were long dead, but their last name was familiar from politics, from old issues of *Semana* and dimly remembered newscasts.

I expected Santander to engage in a shady deal in the quiet of the church. Maybe more Russians. You never knew. I did not expect him to walk to a woman and a child near the nave, the woman too young to be a mother, but the child referring to the woman as mom anyway. Sound carried in Santa Clara. It helped that they all whispered, because the words arrived unencumbered by echoes. Santander asked the woman if everything was all right. The woman said Alejandra just wanted to say hi. She had been asking again about her half sisters. If she could meet them. Santander said, "Someday."

My own grandfather, Camilo Jose's father, long estranged from my grandmother, had a decades-long affair that resulted in five half-siblings for my mother. I thought of those ghostly relations now, trying to remember how I felt about them. They came into our orbit late in my childhood and were first introduced to me as distant cousins.

Santander stood next to his daughter Alejandra and edged away from Alejandra's too-young mother. I was already worried; I had been consumed with worry. My messy past unspooled into the responsible present. I was thinking—I wasn't thinking, I don't know what I was thinking.

"Santander?" I said. "Santander Niebla?"

He turned, and even in the darkness I could tell he was not happy to hear his name. I couldn't tell why I sounded so happy. My wife says that I have a hard time gauging appropriate social cues. That maybe I'm on the spectrum. Maybe I am. But consider, too, that here was a piece of my past. I wanted to see someone who had seen me in shambles, who had seen me as an angry teenage college dropout and could now see me living in the States—respectable, tax-paying, well-groomed.

So I really was happy to see Santander, and (when it was clear he did not remember me) to add, "I used to work for your brother."

He tried to smile. His daughter was all smiles. She said, "Uncle Ricardo."

"I used to work for your uncle," I said.

She held a stuffed raccoon, and it was the raccoon, in a raccoon voice, who replied, "He's been away for a while."

The girl did her best to keep her lips pressed together. An aspiring ventriloquist. In the dark it almost looked like she had it, like she'd mastered it.

Santander put a hand on his daughter's shoulder but said nothing.

"Hi, raccoon," I said.

"Here," she said. She handed me the raccoon.

I wanted to know if he had a name, but she had already pulled out a long, feathered snake from her mom's bag, and her hand was controlling the mouth, and the mouth was saying that she was Aunt Snake, and weren't the paintings beautiful? "There's my cousin," the snake said, pointing to a stiff tableau from Genesis.

I forget what Raccoon said.

It worried me that I hadn't introduced myself, that I knew Santander's name and that they didn't know mine. They didn't know anything about me. I was troubled by how potentially embarrassing the situation could be. For them. How Santander could mistake it for something sinister.

That is why I followed them out the door. Why I said, "You don't understand."

Santander wasn't stopping, he just kept going, herding his secret family in front of him, distinguished in his beautiful double-breasted jacket with its wide lapels, with pick-stitched buttonholes cut into them. I wanted to ask him if he'd bought the blazer in Italy or if he had it made in Colombia. I wanted to let him know that I had a similar blazer in my closet, waiting for me in Pittsburgh. That I'd ordered it off the Web from Banana Republic.

We were already outside, in the gray and the glare of the street, before anyone said anything.

"You don't understand," I said. "I owe your brother money."

Santander turned, his daughter's hand in his own.

"Stop following us," his mistress said—or his former mistress, the mother of his child, at any rate. She pointed at the lonely guard rummaging through an old lady's purse. "We'll call the MP," she said.

You could tell she wouldn't. You could tell that what she really wanted to do was to wrap herself around her child and vanish. Beside her, Alejandra and her snake waved back at me. Untroubled.

I looked at Santander and said, "You don't remember me," but it was the woman who answered, who told me to go to hell, and then they went past the part of the street open to traffic and hailed a cab and I was left holding the girl's stuffed raccoon, the both of us mute.

I spent the rest of the afternoon justifying my behavior to my wife. We also did more sightseeing. We were flying to the coast in two days, to Santa Marta and Tayrona and Palomino, so the window to reconnect with my old self was drawing closed. That's what I told my wife. I told her I needed to know what happened to my former boss.

She said that I didn't. She said that actually I owed no one here anything.

I told her I had failed. I had left intending to be a writer. The novel was a lie, but the truth was I very much intended to write, wanted to write. I was so sure I would. About Colombia, most likely. I told her I had also failed in finding Ricardo. Even if I had not exactly looked that hard, I had at least thought about it—but I had found only his brother.

"They look alike," I said. "They look the same. They look very much alike. So that's something." I told her that Ricardo had gone absent in my absence, and that I wanted to learn what happened to him.

My wife grew quiet. She looked at the raccoon I was holding. She photographed it. She photographed the pigeons in the park.

We sat through the tour about Colombia's independence at La Casa del Florero, whose sole major historical artifact is the broken flower pot it was named after, the same pot that apparently started the revolution, though you learn that it wasn't a flower pot, and that apparently it didn't start it all, not really, and she asked me if I knew this stuff. I did not. That was something else I did not know.

Later that day, when Susanita took my wife to visit friends across town, and when Camilo Jose left to take care of his apartment in Chapinero Bajo, I knocked on Santander's door. He was home. He looked at the raccoon and did not take it when I offered it to him. His other family bustled, unseen— the noise and chatter of a late lunch. He had not invited me in but I understood that it would be unlikely if he did. That it would be awkward. He might find himself having to explain the stuffed animal. His other children were probably teenagers.

"How did you get in?" he said. "You can't come in unless they buzz you in downstairs."

"I'm next door," I said. "I'm visiting. My wife and I are visiting family."

He held the door half open and I caught a peal of laughter. A plate clattered. Steps hustled. I caught a blur of motion inside Santander's apartment: the edge of an orange slipper, a sky-blue apron.

I said, "We don't live here."

He said nothing.

"You don't remember me," I said.

"Of course I remember you," he said, staring at the raccoon.

"I mean from before," I said, "from when I used to work for your brother."

"Of course I remember you," he said again.

I stood there. I wasn't sure I believed him. You'd say anything to rid yourself of a stranger bearing unwelcome news at your doorstep. You'd say anything. And he didn't bring up anything specific about our brief shared experience at the newspaper.

He didn't bring up the Russians. He didn't say, Oh, you were that weird kid who wrote the movie reviews. You were the one who played solitaire on the computer all day. The one who learned PageMaker and did all the layouts when we stopped paying the guy who did the layouts. He didn't remember me. Why should he? His brother's English-language newspaper was just one of many failed enterprises, all more or less indistinguishable, undistinguished.

Santander and I ended up at a cafe by an English-language bookstore that, like the English-language bookstores of my time, charged too much. I didn't care then. I bought books with money I didn't have because I craved print like I craved cigarettes, which I also bought with money I didn't have. And then I discovered this nondenominational expat church's incredible lending library, and through it Rushdie, Roth, Nabokov. When I fled, I fled without returning some of those books. The number that the library called was once again my uncle's. I don't know what happened to their copy of *Ada,* but every used bookstore in Orlando had five fat copies propped in its stacks, and I always thought of buying one and sending it to them, by way of apology.

"My brother's not in jail," Santander said.

"He's not," he said again, as though I didn't believe him. "And he's not back in the States either. He's here. We're just not talking."

We ordered cappuccinos and I heard the story, and I realized that in former days I would have been smoking, and that you couldn't do it freely now, not in the shops in the north, at least.

"This shop's not in my brother's directory," Santander said. He explained. Several years ago, Ricardo had decided to invest in an online directory. He launched a start-up when the whole world launched their start-ups, but he did it wrong, the directory antiquated before it even sputtered online, hopelessly out of date. You could not catalog every store, every tiendita, every type of restaurant that served a fixed-price lunch, not without crowd-sourcing, which wasn't a thing yet. You could not track every tailor in the city. Turn a corner, you'd find five more. And you could not seriously expect any sort of profit from this labor.

"He did," Santander said.

"But not from the cataloguing itself," I said, sure I was right.

Not so. Ricardo hoped that businesses would be willing to pay. To be included. That your ranking would improve according to a shifting scale, so that if you were one of the thirty-four Chinese restaurants in the *centro*, or one of the seventy-six rotisserie joints farther south, you'd pay to be bumped up on the list. To have your name bolded. To have Ricardo include a short, glowing review of your chicken, your *arroz chino*, these reviews supposedly independently arrived at, pre-Yelp yelps of approval, but all delivered in-house. For a fee.

The newspaper money had run out, so now it was just him and, for a while, this one computer-science student from El Externado who worked for free. The student drifted away after a few months. I imagined him being much like me when I worked for Ricardo: lonely, quiet, away from home. Ricardo catalogued Bogota from one small room, using the ancient PCs salvaged from our decommissioned bullpen, their dial-up buzzing and squawking. When I knew him, Ricardo usually had other people do his work for him.

Not now.

Now he walked Bogota, much like I had walked Bogota, and he catalogued everything, he missed nothing. He inventoried the Styrofoam supply company down south, the four floors of the Rojas music supply company, the cevicherias with their pale glasses of clams. He walked the part of Caracas Avenue where prostitutes and mariachis vied for customers by the whiskerias. I had lived in the same city for three years and missed everything, and said as much.

"I don't know this country," I said. "I was born here and lived here for years, but I don't know this country at all."

Santander stayed quiet.

I imagined Ricardo in his double-breasted blazer, perpetually wandering Chapinero at dusk. Still walking Engativá and Fontibón and Los Nogales. Still roaming the streets and noting everything down.

I wanted to ask Santander why he hadn't paid his rent in six months, but I had asked too much already. The in-betweening business must have slowed down. Fewer people kidnapped, maybe. Santander has his own story, but I was interested only in Ricardo's, because for a brief moment it intersected with mine. We were almost done with our coffees. I remembered Ricardo telling me not to drop out of the Javeriana—telling me that I'd have to put up with the dullness of those introductory courses, even though I was clearly bored with them. He said it in a way that made it clear that we were above these petty things. He told me I could succeed. I could be an influential person. I believed him. I believed him when he said that I would end up in some influential think tank as long as I didn't drop out of college. And then I dropped out, and then I flew away. We finished our coffee and I pulled out a wad of dollars. I told Santander they were for Ricardo, for when he saw him. I was sure he wouldn't take it, that it'd be beneath him, but he had no problem doing so, none at all, and I hoped that the money would find its way to his brother. All that I owed was there.

My wife and I flew to the coast the next day, Alejandra's stuffed raccoon in my suitcase.

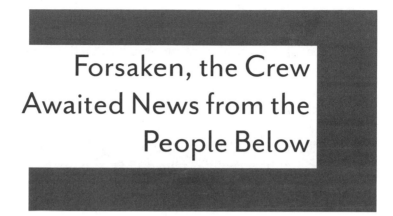

Forsaken, the Crew Awaited News from the People Below

Forsaken, the crew awaited news from the people below. At noon they gathered at the helm. The device was on. They leaned into it, their ears pressed against the auricular, and heard nothing. Stomachs rumbled. Robert mistook the rumbling for the burning of coal, but he was quickly shushed and corrected.

By midnight only five remained. The rest had gone below. The five at the helm waited for news, but heard nothing, not even rumbling stomachs. (Lunch had been served at two: braised goose, Pop-Tarts, fettuccini.) Robert expressed anger, and also (at eight) renewed hunger. He was shushed and reprimanded. They waited, ears close to the auricular on the device, and developed theories.

The theories:

(1) The device was working, else at least one person from the crew would have returned and asked if they

had not heard him, the person returning, speaking through the device—maybe shouting. Maybe even gesticulating, as many do when on the telephone, for no practical reason. But something was keeping them—what it was, nobody knew. But:

(a) It was so interesting that it kept the crew below thoroughly absorbed. All interest in communicating with those above was replaced by interest in this considerably more interesting thing.

(b) It was so deadly that it obliterated the crew before they could use the device. And not only deadly and terrible, but also very very quick, for how else could it get to them before they could even scream?

(2) The device was not working, else they would have heard some sign of it at work. Regardless, as in (1), some force kept them below. So:

(a) As in (1a), though some conceded that maybe even with the interesting thing, the crew would have made some efforts to use the device—perhaps to tell them of the interesting thing. But if it was too fascinating, they agreed, the efforts to communicate via the broken device or to attempt repair were most likely half-hearted.

(b) As in (1b): They had not returned because they had been eaten—or something—by the horrible thing. And they had not heard the screams (and other remonstrations of agony & etc.) because of the malfunctioning device. Unlike (1b), (2b) posited a thing that needed not be devilishly quick. As a variant of which:

(c) The thing itself had disabled the device,

and proceeded to (2b). So the thing did not
need to be possessed of uncanny swiftness,
merely some basic mechanical ability. Or luck:
It might have broken the device by accident.
(3) The crew below were playing a practical joke on
those above. Ha ha. Though of course it was probably terrifically funny once down there—you were "in
the know" the minute you descended. Were there not
muffled chuckles heard through the device? Alas, there
were not. But the device could have been temporarily
disconnected. Ha ha. And the forsaken crew above—
only three remained—would be forced to consider
theoreticals (1a)-(3a), much to the delectation and
hooting of those below. Also maybe:
(a) It had started as a joke, but the presence of
a horrible thing could have led to theoreticals
(2a)-(c).

Forsaken, the three awaited news. Robert complained, and
panicked, and said he was going down there. To which the
other two said, Whatever, fine, do what you will. But he was
just bluffing, the coward.

They reached shore and contacted the maritime authorities. The authorities boarded the ship. They were never seen
again. More authorities boarded, also never to be seen again.

Nobody has since gone into the bowels of the ship.

All passageways leading downwards have been sealed.

Its helm (with the device intact, functioning or not) is
open to the public on Tuesdays and Thursdays, from nine
to five, two dollars for adults, one dollar for children, free
for children under two. Photographs are allowed but not
encouraged.

Most, when photographed, lean into the device, ears
against the auricular. "Hello?" they say in jest. If the crew and

authorities are still down there, and the device is functioning from their end, that's all they hear: Hello, hello, hello. Hello, anybody there? Hello?

Northern

Marta Helena, our houseguest, wants to know why my wife Elisia screams at night. We are reluctant to tell her.

Elisia springs from our bed, screams, points to an empty spot in the room, and usually that is all. Tonight, however, she runs into the guest bedroom and holds on to Marta Helena's ankles and will not stop screaming. Elisia tore down our poster of Gustav Dasa. She wears a promotional T-shirt misspelling our place of employment, which is also what Marta Helena and I wear. The sound that Elisia makes is not high, not screechy—her scream is long and loud and deep-throated and it will not stop. It is two in the morning on my night off, and I was only now about to drift into sleep after struggling as I always do with the nocturnal habits of others (usually I am up at this hour). If we had any neighbors, the sound would carry in the dead of the Summerlin air and they would wake up.

"I don't know if I should wake her," Marta Helena says. I can hear her, though she is whispering, and though my wife's screaming has not stopped. "Should I wake her?"

I say nothing. It should be clear to Marta Helena that all we need to do is wait, so I sit on the guest bed close to my wife and wait. This close, this loud, my wife's sound carries enough weight to hurt.

Marta Helena puts her hands against her ears. I just wait. I wait, and I abide.

We were not underwater, though if we had been it would not have made a difference. The stories grew around the edges of our marriage, and from the stories our trouble. Everyone else was in trouble—stressed in all senses of the word and owing mysterious entities money. How we managed to avoid even so much as a spike in our mortgage when the crisis took its last nightmare turn, I don't know, and neither did Elisia. We soldiered on in silence, not talking about it, as though talking about it would have somehow broken the spell and brought the mess of Vegas into our lives.

We did not say anything to our friends or our co-workers because doing so felt indecorous. We also didn't say anything because it would be sure to trigger their own tales of woe, and we were all sick of them, as I'm sure you are, surrounded on every side by this endless stream of misery and discontent and anger. We stayed silent.

"You don't talk much," Marta Helena says. At the time of the first problems she was Elisia's friend, the erstwhile owner of two houses and one condo. "You're not angry, are you?"

She spoke to both of us. I shook my head. Elisia continued her screaming.

Our houseguest came originally from Guanajuato, as did Elisia, but Elisia's Guanajuato is by way of Skåne County, which is where we met (though I'm Venezuelan originally, not Mexican), and Marta Helena came to Vegas by way of Pasadena, and her folks were originally from Guanajuato. But if you were to ask her (we did not, others did), Marta Helena, where are you from? She'd say, Guanajuato. Which I did not understand.

I said to Elisia, Why doesn't she say Pasadena? I said, You are from the place where you are born or the place you lived the most. Elisia said, Who are you, Donald Trump? Then she said, We never say we are from Sweden. To which I would have said, Because it is too complicated. So Marta Helena is from Guanajuato, by way of Pasadena. And she does not know where we are from.

You wouldn't know it was Sweden, though, and you wouldn't really need to know it, and truth be told no one really understands the large and for the most part fairly prosperous Hispanic community in Scandia.

We joke about putting lingonberries in the ajis and the pico de gallos, but then we also do actually put them in there, and the truth is they work.

Marta Helena speaks too much. We put up with it because we understand that some people are made uncomfortable by silence. But we do not feel obligated to fill that silence ourselves.

We do not talk much. I work the graveyard shift as a line cook, Elisia a more regular morning and afternoon turn as a maid—both of us at the Fitzgerald's on Freemont, and both of us too long there and too entrenched in the union to worry. We are lucky. We know that we are lucky. Our marriage is neither troubled nor untroubled, our house purchased at the sweetest possible spot with a significant down payment after years of toil and sensible choices. (This too we kept from those who knew us.) Vegas was crazed but we were sane, and being sane we stayed silent.

The house overlooks the vast lake of small rocks and defeated scrub that edges out into the red rock range. It is newly built—not big, not small, too overly furnished with marble for our taste. We were the only people occupying a house in our particular subdivision. The developer painted the houses in ochres and umbers designed to blend with the desert, which we liked after our time in Scandia. We liked the warmth, the absence of snow, the winding Summerlin roads keeping our particular rounded corner of the world invisible from the bustle of Charleston and the looming presence of the Stratosphere.

"Have you thought about what I said?" Marta Helena says. "About the money? Please don't tell your wife." I try to look anywhere but at Marta Helena. "She can't hear me, can she? Us?"

From where we sit, through the window, we can make out one lonely truck in the moonlight. During the day it moves gravel about, readying another lot for another set of empty houses.

"Maybe I could just, you know, sleep over there," Marta Helena says. She shakes her hair at the house next door, where the yard is overgrown, though no one has watered it. "Just shower and stuff here. Who would know?"

"You are welcome here for as long as you need to be here," I say.

"We don't want you to get into any trouble," Elisia says. "Who knows what could happen? Maybe someone calls the cops. Maybe there's already squatters. Drug users. Criminals. Homeless people. Stay here."

"Kidding!" Marta Helena says. "Geez."

It is three in the afternoon and it is July, so the sun is paralyzing. We are outside, grilling salmon, under a promotional Coca-Cola tarpaulin we found in a garage sale. We are eating dinner because it is the only time that me and Elisia share, other than a few hours of mostly interrupted sleep. We keep thinking about asking for a change in schedule but never get around to it. It is my suspicion that we both feel this particular arrangement works best. We each get the house to ourselves. Of course it will have to be different when we have children.

"Also, *I'm* homeless," Marta Helena says.

We tell her that she's not, and she says once more that she's kidding, though we don't really think she is.

Marta Helena's face is as round and as taut and as pale as last night's moon. She worked the same shift as Elisia for two years, covered for Elisia on the three days after my wife's miscarriage (about which my wife never confided in Marta Helena), and was fired when she failed a drug test. She has not found a job. She takes the bus to the Green Valley library (she never learned how to drive) and looks for openings on job boards and Craigslist, but nothing has surfaced, she tells us, and she has no intention of going back to her family in Pasadena because of some issues with her father. She was taking some computer courses but then they shut those down because of the budget. Some of this I know because she tells it to us. Some of this I know because she tells it to her friends—none of whom, we've made it clear, are welcome in the house—when she is on the phone, as she is now, while my wife and I finish our salmon. We do not talk about when Marta Helena should leave, but it is fair to say that she should leave sooner rather than later.

"No, I'm telling you. I'm telling you," Marta Helena says to one of her invisible friends. "I was like, You cannot treat me this way. I am not a moron like the rest of these morons here."

Elisia walks back into the house with our plates. It is almost time for her afternoon shift. Inside, I know that she is putting the dishes in the dishwasher and that she will then go upstairs and change into her work clothes. (She dislikes and thus avoids the staff lockerroom at the Fitzgerald's.) There is a pleasure in knowing your mate—in knowing what she is up to, in anticipating the familiar, in dividing one's day and one's life into known and predictable segments. I think of routines and subroutines, of my work as a machine-language programmer before settling on the far more tasking (but inexplicably far more rewarding) demands of prepping and cooking a nearly endless stream of consistent omelets.

"I *know*. Shut up. I know. All right? I know." Marta Helena does not stop talking on the cell phone. She lowers her shorts and pulls her underwear in so I can see her ass. "What do you think?" She cups the phone with one hand. "He said it'd be $2,500 down, $3,000 later."

I finish my salmon. I do not tell her what I think. What I think is, My wife is upstairs. My wife, who I love very much, would not appreciate you disrobing in front of me. But of course I do not say anything. Because the problem is that there are lots more things that Marta Helena could say to my wife that she would appreciate even less.

"You should not have slept with me," Marta Helena says.

About that much we are in agreement. About the money, which she wants for plastic surgery that would (she claims) kick-start a long-dormant modeling career—not so much.

My wife returns in a maid uniform that neither flatters nor detracts from her essential loveliness. Her essential decency. "What did I miss?" she says.

"Marta Helena showed me her ass," I say.

Elisia laughs. "Yes! The modeling thing."

Marta Helena's usually pale face turns a deep brown.

I think, You don't know us. You don't know me and my wife at all, do you?

That night work is beastly and the long and uninterrupted chain of orders and ingredients somehow goes, as these things sometimes do, without a hitch, a symphony of meaningful noise, all of us shouting clearly and responding just as clearly, all of us one organism—and all of it in Spanish ranging from excellent to fair, even down to the two *gueros* on staff. *Guero* doesn't really mean anything where I'm from, but you adopt. You adopt and you adapt. However, *guero* sounds awfully familiar, because Venezuela has *catira-guey*, a fake blonde, which inevitably leads to me thinking about Marta Helena, whose hair has the tired scraggly look of our landscaping—harsh, brittle, chemically treated. I grow hard. I think of her softness, and also of her roundness and her blitheness. It is the blitheness that gets me. You think, Who would go to bed with that ditz? And then it turns out to be you.

The whole week goes by, blithely.

I avoid Marta Helena. I hardly see my wife.

When I do see my wife, she tells me she is worried about Marta Helena, that she doesn't look too good. My wife is as cheerful as ever.

When I do see Marta Helena (inevitable, given that we live in the same house), I find my wife's judgement to be correct: Marta Helena doesn't look too good. Her face is paler than usual, and sweaty, and blotchy. She coughs. She sees me one time in the corridor and walks toward me, but her gait is off. She's slow, she leans against our new walls, she inadvertently wrinkles the Dasa poster.

"About the money—" she says.

I don't hear the rest. I remain silent and glide quietly to better things.

One day, our entire prep staff vanishes (we suspect hangover), so I spend most of the afternoon chopping onions into precise and minute cubes no bigger than rain drops. I see the face of my wife: She has the high cheekbones of Skandia and the dark skin of the P'urhépecha. Her eyes are green in sunlight and metallic in photographs. No red-eye correction that we know of can fix this irregularity, which shows up more often than you'd think in our women.

You'll find a lost tribe of Germans living in Venezuela. It's mostly a tourist attraction these days, but it's real—the Colonia Tovar. I look at all of us here and think, that's what we are. We're a Colonia Tovar in reverse.

We never talk about going back to Skåne County. Why would we? We carry the place with us.

My wife screams. She springs from our bed, screams, and points to a empty spot in the room. "Who is that? Who is that?" she says. "What's it doing here?"

It is my night off. I cannot say I am ready for this, but I cannot say that I am not.

"Shut her up," Marta Helena says. She leans against the bedroom door, has been there for who knows how long (my wife has been screaming for a long time), her face a sickly white, her skin damp. Her dead hair sticks to her scalp. "I swear to God I'll tell her. I'm not a moron like you morons here. I swear to God." She holds a scrap of glossy paper from which I can make out a man's mouth and moustache. "Who the fuck is this guy? Shut her up."

"Who is that? Who is that?" my wife says, pointing to the same empty corner of our bedroom.

Marta Helena has torn down our poster of Gustav Dasa. She does not look like she's in good shape. She had problems with drugs before, but she knows that we'll kick her out if she brings drugs into the house. We have told her as much. We don't say much, but we've made that clear. "Shut her up," she says.

I do not. My wife does not stop screaming.

"I need help," Marta Helena says. "I need you to take me to a hospital. I need you to shut her up and to take me to a hospital."

She pulls down her sweat pants. Her ass is horribly infected, visible even in this light: puffs of skin the color and wetness of chicken fat bubble out of her cheeks. A few have popped and what suppurates is yellow and red, some of it liquid, some of it still streaming, some of it coagulated and already scabbing, already filling up again with more liquid. The stench is powerful. From across the room I can smell it. Rot. Sweet and awful. The infection is a whole territory, a topography of pain and repulsion. I think, I touched that ass. I think, This is what our bodies to do us.

Marta Helena falls to the floor, her ass in the air. "Shut her up," she says. "Please. Please shut her up."

I say nothing. My wife screams, "Who's there?"

"You should have given me the money. I'll tell her. I swear to God I'll tell her," Marta Helena says. "I'm not a moron."

It will be a week later that we get the full story from the police. Days before, Marta Helena had gone to a botanica on Charleston where—past the candles to the saints and past the packets of herbs and the international calling cards and the cheaply printed pamphlets with spells for attracting love and money—you could find unlicensed doctors willing to operate for vastly reduced fees. Even then, we later found out, she could not round up the money herself. Marta Helena made off with our emergency fund—we keep a secondary savings account for a real emergency, of course, but we also kept a small amount of cash in the house, just in case, in a small cedar box nestled in the little nook we usually obscure behind the thumbtacked poster of Gustav Dasa.

Elisia says, "All in all, not the best of hiding places."

I cannot say. I thought it was fine. You don't think you'd have guests rummaging where they shouldn't.

The police will inform us that Marta Helena died of her infections. They find her in a lot far from our neighborhood, but they of course have their suspicions. But we did file the report ourselves. And we can say, with total honesty, that we have no idea how she ended up in that lot—though of course we have our suspicions too. Marta Helena's death is a long process. It takes her days to die—she was well on her way when she made her way to the bedroom door that night. The police investigation will also be a long process, it will take months, and they will have (as I just told you) their suspicions, but it will ultimately work out all right—not pleasant, but not too terrible, all things considered. They ask us (they will keep asking us), Did you know something was wrong? We tell them the truth. We say, Yes. Yes, we knew something was wrong.

But of course we don't tell them everything.

"Who's there?" my wife says.

This time it is Marta Helena who screams. She pulls herself from the floor and points at the same corner my wife is pointing at and says, "What is that?"

I do not tell her. I do not explain to her that it is our child—Elisia's, properly speaking, but really mine and Elisia's and Marta Helena's. We are all responsible for it. Our child stands at a full three feet. (I've measured others before and will measure this one too: they all stand a full three feet.) Its skin is glossy and wet and pale black and covered in small profuse pockmarks. It has no eyes, no nose, no sexual organs. It opens its mouth to reveal long jagged teeth and the wet healthy pink tongue of an infant.

"What is that?" Marta Helena says. "What does it want?"

I do not tell her that it wants to kill us. I do not tell her that my wife, for whatever reason, conjures these creatures from her troubled sleep and from whatever rage is triggered by the world—by the world and by the people in it and mostly, I suspect, by the infelicities and faults of her husband. I say nothing by way of explanation to Marta Helena. She does not deserve an explanation. I simply walk over to my child and snap its neck.

"There will be others," I say. "It is better if you go to your room and lock your door."

"You need to take me to the hospital," Marta Helena says.

I cannot go anywhere. I cannot leave the neighborhood until the children are taken care of.

It is only after I've snapped the neck of the fourth child that I notice that Marta Helena is no longer in the room. My wife has stopped screaming, so all should be well.

The guest room is open, as is our front door.

She stands outside in the moonlight. She has not put her pants back on and she has not stopped screaming, but there is no one to be bothered here by her immodesty or by her infected wounds or by her voice. "Please help," she says. She cries.

She follows me into the adjacent house. "Please," she says. "I'm not—"

"You need to leave," I say. "You need to go back to our house and go into your room and lock your door."

"I'm not well," Marta Helena says, "I'm not—"

She does not say whatever she was going to say. (Moron, I think. I am not one of those morons like those other morons, is what I think she was going to say.) The words stop when she sees the living room stuffed to the ceiling with the wet black bodies of our children. The house is full of them, the house is choking with them.

Do not ask me why I simply left her there.

Do not ask me why I realized, that night, that you would take care of the problem. We share the same blood, you and I. You are my own—you are all my own. Mine and Elisia's.

The truth is that I'm glad to see you all tonight.

The truth is that I do not want to know how you managed to carry her body, you're all so small.

The truth is that I do not regret having killed so many of you. Look: Every house in this block is stuffed with the bodies of your brethren, all of them the same, all of them like you. No one comes around. This whole subdivision blooms with corpses. No one looks in the empty houses, and so they remain empty. If they were to find you I don't know what they would say, what they would make of you. I don't think they could make anything of you. What you are. Why you are here.

The police looked, you know. They looked around this neighborhood. They could not find you.

But I am glad to see you tonight, because tomorrow Elisia will smile at me, no matter what horrible things I've done, what horrible things I carry with me. My beautiful wife will smile at me and we'll have our time together, like we always do, and all will be forgiven because all will be forgotten. We will spend tomorrow, like we will spend the rest of our life, in bliss and silence.

Best Worst American

Later is time for explanation—now is just time for looking bad, for looking like man in expensive suit chasing heavyset woman in the flapping navy Wal-Mart vest across the vast prairie of the Wal-Mart. So for clarification: suit not so expensive, only looks expensive, looks not so expensive. What? Is bad spy movie, is Rocky and Bullwinkle, Boris and Natasha. So he is no Russian, the woman no Natasha. He wants to say to woman, Wait! Wait! But he does not, he walk fast and the woman walk faster.

Is as a child—not now—he narrate adventures in heavy Russian accent. Matthew goes to sidewalk on the bike even though he is not supposed to be on bike but is SECRET MIS-SION. Is OK. Soon is revealed, all is forgotten, mom forgives, all is acceptable. Is as child, not now. So why now?

They cross great aisles: bouquets of hardware, wildernesses of Schwinn bikes, topiaries of grills, Great Walls of China of produce and electronics and socks. Is discreet chase. No running. Just furious furious walking.

Is her. Is her. She stops. She turns around. He'd seen her as a kid, on Oprah, in that episode on child prodigies: He'd seen her perform a complicated musical piece on the piccolo, then paint a portrait of Oprah using crayons that was just way way better than anything a five-year-old should do. He'd been watching at home, a slacker teenager, and he was seriously stoned, but he remembered her, remembered those eyes, remembered the scar that ran across her face. A child of the Ukraine. Abused at an orphanage. Before orphanage: Alcoholic parents. What else? All the expected elses.

Look at her, Oprah had said. Is story of perseverance, hope.

He does not want to ask what happened. He just wants to tell her that she saved his life: He'd been adrift and he'd seen her on TV and he'd turned his life around. He wants to tell her that his life had been pointless and undisciplined and then—that day, because of her—things had turned around, had gotten better. There'd been hope, perseverance. If the Ukrainian girl did it, he thought, why not him?

They stand by a river of refrigerated meat.

"Can I help you with anything?" she says.

He moves to hug her, and he sees her flinch, but he can't help himself. She says, "What's wrong with you?" but she's hugging him back. "This happens," she says, "Sometimes. You don't realize how many people see that show." Her accent has faded, but it's still there.

He nods, then remembers. He'd looked it up. "Дякую," he says.

"Прошу," she says, not letting go, neither one letting go.

Publication History

"Roadblock" and "Well Tended" originally appeared in *Glimmer Train*.

"Strangers on Vacation: Snapshots," "The Lead Singer Is Distracting Me," "The Spooky Japanese Girl Is There for You," "After the End of the World: A Capsule Review," and "Forsaken, the Crew Awaited News from the People Below" originally appeared in *McSweeney's*.

"Customer Service at the Karaoke Don Quixote" originally appeared in *McSweeney's*, was reprinted in *Norton's Sudden Fiction Latino*, and was broadcast on National Public Radio's *Selected Shorts*.

"Machulín in L.A." originally appeared in the *Santa Monica Review*.

"On Paradise" originally appeared in *The Perpetual Engine of Hope: Stories Inspired by Iconic Las Vegas Photographs*.

"Domokun in Fremont" originally appeared in *TriQuarterly.*

"The Women Who Talk to Themselves," "Errands," and "My Sister's Knees" originally appeared in *Pindeldyboz.*

"Your Significant Other's Kitten Poster" and "Liner Notes for Renegade, the Opening Sequence" originally appeared in *Sceal.*

"Souvenirs from Ganymede" originally appeared in *River Teeth.*

"The Coca-Cola Executive in the Zapatoca Outhouse" originally appeared in *Conjunctions.*

"Correspondences between the Lower World and Old Men in Pinstripe Suits" originally appeared in *Interim.*

"Hobbledehoydom" originally appeared in the *Morning News.*

"Debtor" originally appeared in *Ecotone.*

"Northern" originally appeared in *Huizache: the Magazine of Latino Literature.*

"Best Worst American" was commissioned by and originally broadcast on National Public Radio's *Selected Shorts,* and was performed by Cristin Milioti.

Acknowledgments

Big hugs & love to Sarah & Saúl & giant thanks to agent/gentleman Jim Rutland & editors Gavin J. Grant & Kelly Link & to all the journal editors (Linda Swanson-Davies & Susan Burmeister-Brown of *Glimmer Train*, Kevin Shay & John Warner & Jordan Bass of *McSweeney's*, Andrew Tonkovich of *Santa Monica Review*, Geoff Schumaker & Scott Dickensheets of Stephens Press, Jeff Boison & Whitney Pastorek of *Pindeldyboz*, Tigernan Pournelle of *Sceal*, Joe Mackall of *River Teeth*, Micaela Morrissette & Bradford Morrow of *Conjunctions*, Claudia Keelan & Christopher Arigo of *Interim*, Diana López & Dagoberto Gilb of *Huizache*, Jennifer Brennan & Katherine Minton of *Selected Shorts*) & to all the colleagues & peeps & students at Whitman College & Lebanon Valley College & Northwestern University & dear friends near & far away. You know who you are.

About the Author

Juan Martinez was born in Bucaramanga, Colombia, and has since lived in Orlando, Florida, and Las Vegas, Nevada. He now lives in Chicago with his wife, the writer Sarah Kokernot, and their son and two cats. He's an assistant professor at Northwestern University. His work has appeared in various literary journals and anthologies, including *Glimmer Train, McSweeney's, Ecotone, Huizache, TriQuarterly, Conjunctions,* the *Cossack Review,* the *Santa Monica Review,* National Public Radio's Selected Shorts, Norton's *Sudden Fiction Latino,* and elsewhere. Visit and say hi at fulmerford.com.